THE Listening Tree

WITHDRAWN

Celia Barker Lottridge

Fitzhenry & Whiteside
www.fitzhenry.ca

THE Listening Tree

Celia Barker Lottridge

Published in Canada by Fitzhenry & Whiteside,
195 Allstate Parkway, Markham, Ontario L3R 4T8

Published in the United States by Fitzhenry & Whiteside,
311 Washington Street, Brighton, Massachusetts 02135

10 9 8 7 6 5 4 3 2 1

Library and Archives Canada Cataloguing in Publication
Lottridge, Celia B. (Celia Barker)
The listening tree / Celia Barker Lottridge.
ISBN 978-1-55455-052-4
I. Title.
PS8573.O855L68 2010   jC813'.54   C2010-904389-8

U.S. Publisher Cataloging-in-Publication Data (Library of Congress Standards)
Lottridge, Celia Barker.
The listening tree / Celia Barker Lottridge.
[160] p. : cm.
ISBN-13: 978-1-55455-052-4
1. Interpersonal relations – Juvenile fiction. 2. Self-esteem – Juvenile fiction.
3. Courage – Juvenile fiction. I. Title.
[Fic]. dc22   PZ7.L68847Li 2010

Fitzhenry & Whiteside acknowledges with thanks the Canada Council for the Arts, and
the Ontario Arts Council for their support of our publishing program. We acknowledge
the financial support of the Government of Canada through the Book Publishing
Industry Development Program (BPIDP) for our publishing activities.

 Canada Council   Conseil des Arts   ONTARIO ARTS COUNCIL
for the Arts   du Canada   CONSEIL DES ARTS DE L'ONTARIO

Cover and interior design by Kerry Designs
Printed in Canada

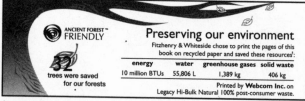

Preserving our environment

Fitzhenry & Whiteside chose to print the pages of this
book on recycled paper and saved these resources[1]:

energy	water	greenhouse gases	solid waste
10 million BTUs	55,806 L	1,389 kg	406 kg

trees were saved
for our forests

Printed by Webcom Inc. on
Legacy Hi-Bulk Natural 100% post-consumer waste.

[1]Estimates were made using the Environmental Defense Paper Calculator.

FSC

Mixed Sources
Product group from well-managed
forests, controlled sources and
recycled wood or fiber

Cert no. SW-COC-002358
www.fsc.org
© 1996 Forest Stewardship Council

For Jonathan and Nancy and everyone at 220 long ago.

CHAPTER 1

Ellen looked down the railroad track. She could see her father not far away, standing with a group of other men. They wore heavy jackets and boots, and each one carried a canvas bag. They were waiting for a train. Not the passenger train that would pull up to the Moose Jaw station but a freight train. It would stop out here, in the rail yard.

Ellen kicked at a stone and a little cloud of dust rose up. Dust. That was the whole problem. There had been almost no rain for so long that Ellen could barely remember the sound of rain on the roof. And now, in November, there was no snow.

Mama called it "the everlasting drought," and that drought was the reason Dad was hopping a freight and going west.

"After all our hard work this past summer, we have nothing." That was what he'd said to Mama and Ellen just last week. "This part of Saskatchewan is nothing but dust. Well, I'm not waiting for rain any longer. A bunch of us who farm around here are getting on the freight train when it goes through next Saturday. They say there are jobs out west for men who aren't afraid of hard work. I have to try. I'll send money as soon as I can."

So that was that. He hadn't wanted Mama and Ellen to see him off, but Mama didn't listen.

"You're not running away, Mike," she said. "You're going to find work so we won't starve. That's what you have to do and we'll be there to wave goodbye."

Now Ellen could hear the train in the distance, and moments later she could see the smoke flowing behind the engine as it rumbled toward them.

It wasn't a very long train. Not much was being shipped by rail during these hard times. The men who were waiting ran along the track as the train slowed down, looking up at the closed doors of freight cars. One slid open as the train stopped, and Ellen could see that there were men inside. They reached down and caught the hands of the men outside to pull them up into the freight car.

Dad was the last man up and he stood in the doorway and looked toward Mama and Ellen. Ellen waved as hard as she could and Dad pulled off his hat and waved to her and to Mama. Then someone inside pushed the door shut.

Mama looked at the closed door for a moment. Then she took Ellen's hand and said, "We might as well go home. There's no more to see."

When they got home Mama made tea from the precious

tin of tea leaves she kept for special occasions.

"This is one of those times when we need a little comfort," she said to Ellen. "We'll save the rest of the tea for the day your dad writes that he has a job. That could be a long time, but I want you to know that while we wait for news we have enough money from selling the cattle to get you and me through the winter. We'll eat a lot of beans and oatmeal but we'll survive. So don't worry."

Ellen did worry, of course. Not about getting through the winter, but about Dad. Every day when she came home from school she hoped that Mr. Carson, their neighbour down the road, would have come from town with a letter. She heard all sorts of things from the kids at school about the men who had gone to look for work. They were living in camps by the railroad. They were in jail. They were working in the mountains or in a shipyard. But where was her dad? All she could see when she thought of him was that freightcar door closing.

Month after month, nothing came. Then on a bright day in March, Mama met Ellen at the kitchen door with a letter in her hand.

"It's pretty good news," she said. "Sit down. I want to read it to you."

I've been in the back country here in British Columbia and haven't been able to get a letter out at all. I'm sorry. I think about you two all the time. I couldn't find any work at first, but for now I have a job in a logging camp. I'm glad I can finally send you some money. I hope it's in time to keep you from going broke. Two dollars are for you, Ellen. I know you've been helping your mama all you can. Wish me luck that this work keeps up.

Mama looked up from the letter. "It's been hard to think of your father with no work to do. All his life, he's taken care of this farm. He'll be so glad to be working again and we really need this money."

She gave the two one-dollar bills to Ellen and, true to her word, filled up the kettle and made a pot of tea.

Ellen folded her bills carefully and put them safely in her pocket. She thought of Dad surrounded by tall trees, swinging an axe. It was better than remembering the freight car, but she wished for another letter that would tell her more. Where did he sleep at night? Did he cook for himself over a fire? Were any of his friends from home with him?

A month passed, then another. School closed for the summer, and still no letter came.

CHAPTER 2

Ellen lay in bed waiting to hear the whistle of the night train. She knew it was an eastbound train coming from British Columbia, headed for Regina, Winnipeg, and Toronto. Every night as she listened, she told herself that one day her dad would jump off that train at Moose Jaw and come home.

The hot air lay over Ellen like a blanket, and she could feel sweat trickle from her upper lip into the corner of her mouth. For once, the wind wasn't blowing. Most nights it swept over the little wooden house, driving dust and grit into every crack, but tonight the wind was still.

Hot as she was, Ellen was nearly asleep when she heard the whistle, starting low and then rising to pierce through the night. She knew that the train had a light that shone down the track in front of it, but the sound of the whistle traveled even farther, crossing fields and dry stream beds, sweeping over houses and barns and dried-up fields. She hoped that her dad could hear a train whistle wherever he was.

Before she could start thinking of him cooking over a lonely campfire, Ellen made herself fall asleep.

She woke up to another sunny, dusty day. She knew that

breakfast would be oatmeal made out of the oats that were left when Mama sold their last horse, Chief. When Mr. Carson came to take the big brown horse away, he'd asked for any feed that was left.

Mama said, "I've sold you the last of the livestock from this farm, Jack. The oats stay here. People can eat oats, you know."

Mr. Carson shook his head. "If you're down to eating oats, Martha, maybe you should think about leaving. You don't know when Mike will be back. Not for a long time, maybe. Don't you have some family somewhere back east?"

Mama didn't answer and Ellen saw that her mouth was set in the stubborn line she knew so well. Mama was determined to stay on the farm until Dad came back, but Ellen knew that she spent hours sitting at the kitchen table, looking over bills, and then staring out the window.

"There's not much to do around here but sweep the dust out the door," she said to Ellen one day, and she sighed.

It was true. There wasn't much to do around the farm. The cattle and horses were gone, and everything in the garden the two of them had planted in the spring had dried up for lack of rain. Only the chickens were left. They lived by scratching in the dirt and eating grasshoppers. Once in a while, one of them managed to lay an egg.

This morning, Ellen sat down ready to eat rough oatmeal,

but her mother set a scrambled egg and an oatcake in front of her instead. And a cup of tea. It looked very good but Ellen was puzzled. If they were lucky enough to have an egg, they always ate it for supper. She looked up from the plate to see her mother watching her with her eyebrows raised, waiting for her reaction.

"I wanted to surprise you," she said. "Lately, every day has been the same. Oatmeal and no rain. I can't make it rain, but it's a pleasure to give you a good breakfast for once. And maybe it will help you take in a bigger surprise."

"A surprise?" asked Ellen. From Mama's tone of voice, she was pretty sure it wasn't going to be a good surprise.

"Yes," said Mama. "It's a surprise to me too, but I've decided that Jack Carson is right. You and I can't stay here eating oats, and that means leaving the farm for a while."

Ellen stared at Mama and then gazed around the familiar kitchen.

"But if we go, the house will be empty," she said. "When Dad comes back he won't find us here. He can't even write us a letter if he doesn't know where we are."

"I don't think Mike will be back for a while. Not this summer for sure. And Jack will know where we are. He'll send on Mike's letters."

Mama sat down and took Ellen's hand and squeezed it. Her brow creased with worry. "I just hope your dad will find a place where he can settle down and work. Then we can write to him and tell him what we're doing. We have to remember that we're luckier than many people in this Depression. We own our land and we didn't borrow money, so the bank won't get our farm. And when it starts raining again, we'll come back. All of us."

She got up, walked over to the window, and looked out at the dirt patch where the garden used to be. Then she turned back to Ellen.

"You and I can't wait any longer. I have just enough left from the money Mike sent in March to buy us two tickets to Toronto."

"Toronto?" All Ellen could think of was pictures in her geography book of a big city with tall buildings and cars crowding the streets. She had never seen a picture of houses in Toronto.

"Where can we live in Toronto? And how can we go without money?" Ellen could see that Mama had made up her mind. But surely this decision was a mistake.

Mama sat down at the table again. "I'll tell you the whole plan, but there's no use arguing because we have no choice. We have to go. You know that my big sister Gladys lives in Toronto. Well, months ago, after Mike left, she wrote and asked the two of us to come and live with her. She has a boarding house and she'll give us a room and our meals if I help her with the cooking and such. I know you've never met Gladys but she's dying to see you. You still have the doll she sent you one Christmas, don't you?"

Ellen nodded. To her, Aunt Gladys was just a little figure in some photographs, not a real person. Then she took in what Mama had said. "A boarding house? That means a lot of people living in rooms, doesn't it?"

"Yes, and eating breakfast and dinner together. We won't be lonely."

The thought of sitting down to eat with a table full of strangers did not comfort Ellen.

She looked straight at Mama. "You never told me that we might leave. I thought we were managing. And going all the way to Toronto! I never thought of anything like that."

Her mother picked up her teacup and put it down. Then she said, "I didn't want to think about leaving the farm either, so I didn't talk about it to anyone. Even you. I just pretended it would never be necessary. But now I know that it *is* necessary. We can't stay here and starve. We need help and your Aunt Gladys has offered to help us. And we'll help her, too. We won't be charity. I should be able to get a job. I've been told there are jobs in Toronto. Here, there is nothing."

She looked toward the window. "Ellen, can you remember when we had green fields and a beautiful garden and a cow that gave milk?"

Ellen nodded. "I remember picking peas and shelling them and eating them right in the garden. And you let me plant some flowers of my own."

"I'm glad you remember because you were only four or five when the rain stopped and the land began to blow away. That was 1930. Now it's 1934 and you're nine years old. These hard times have taken up such a big part of your life. We've held on long enough. Maybe Mike will find some kind of work wherever he is. That's what I hope for every day."

She stood up. "As for you and me, we're going to Toronto. And I guarantee you that we won't be eating oatmeal morning, noon, and night. Now, eat your egg. We have packing to do."

CHAPTER 3

The next two days passed in a blur. Mama gave Ellen a cardboard suitcase not much bigger than her pillow.

"This should hold the clothes that still fit you," she said. "You can pack the things you want to leave here in the trunk in your room. Everything that's too small, I'll take to the church. Somebody can use it."

Ellen laid the doll Aunt Gladys had sent her when she was a little girl carefully in the trunk along with her other baby toys and most of the books on her shelf. She saved *Anne of Green Gables* to take with her. She had read it three times, but she couldn't imagine not having it nearby.

Her clothes went into two piles: too-small and big-enough. The too-small pile was taller. Mama said that on her ninth birthday in February, Ellen had started to grow like crazy. Now, in July, she was a good two inches taller and most of her clothes were too short and too skimpy.

In the big-enough pile she put two dresses: one made of blue seersucker and the other of red-checked cotton. And she had a pair of shorts, two cotton shirts, and the shirt and pants she was wearing.

"Should I take my shorts to Toronto?" Ellen asked Mama. "Do you think city girls wear shorts?"

"You'd better take everything that fits," said Mama. "We won't be able to buy anything for a while. I don't know just what I'll do for ready money. We'll have a roof over our heads and food to eat, but until I can get a job, there will be no money for clothes or anything else."

She looked at her own suitcase and made a face.

"I only have three dresses that are good enough for Toronto. It's discouraging. Gladys is going to think we're a pretty raggedy pair. She never did like the idea that I married a farmer and left Regina. She was already married to a fellow who worked in the bank, and a year or two later they up and moved to Toronto. I haven't seen her since, and her husband died just when times got bad. She's on her own now. I guess that's why she turned their big house into a boarding house."

She closed her suitcase with a snap and gave Ellen a little smile.

"Don't worry. When I sent Gladys a telegram saying that you and I were coming, she answered right away. Just one word: 'Come!' With an exclamation mark. So I guess she'll take us just the way we are."

Mr. Carson came the next morning in his Ford pickup truck. He put their two suitcases in the back, and Mama and Ellen squeezed beside him into the cab of the truck.

Ellen kept her school bag on her lap. It contained *Anne of Green Gables*, a scribbler in case she wanted to write or draw pictures, two pencils and a pencil sharpener, and at the very bottom, the dollar bills her dad had sent.

As the truck bumped down the lane that led to the road, Ellen suddenly thought of her best friend, Sarah. The two of them were the only girls in their class at North Star School, and they had known each other forever. She couldn't leave without saying goodbye.

She turned to her mother and asked urgently, "Do we have time to stop at the Murrays' place? I haven't even told Sarah that we're going."

"Just for a minute," said Mama. "Lucky it's right on the way. But we don't want to miss the train."

Sarah was still at the breakfast table when Ellen rushed in.

"What are you doing here so early? And why are you wearing those shoes?" she asked.

Ellen looked down. She was wearing her good shoes, shiny and black with a strap, instead of her usual scuffed brown ones. These ones pinched a little.

"Oh, Sarah," she said. "Mama and I are taking the train to Toronto to live with Aunt Gladys. We can't stay on the farm any more."

Of course Sarah understood. Her father worked on the road-building crew some of the time, hoping he could make it through the drought. But many people were leaving.

"Do you think you'll be back when school starts in September?" she asked. "Will you *ever* come back?"

"I don't know about September, but I'm sure I'll come back. We have the farm, you know, and Mama says the drought won't last forever."

"Ellen! It's time to go!" It was Mama's voice.

"I'll write to you. I promise," said Ellen. Then she pushed open the screen door. She didn't look back because she didn't want to cry.

The train trip to Toronto took three days. Ellen heard the train whistle more times than she could count. She and Mama shared a prickly seat that Mama said was about as comfortable as a church pew. Passengers were passing magazines around, but with the train swaying it was hard to read, so Ellen watched the scenery go by.

For a while, she was looking at familiar prairie land covered in a haze of dust, then at trees and rocks, whipping past the window. Now and then they stopped at a station, and at every station more and more of the seats in the car were filled.

They left the open land behind and passed little groups of cabins and lakes and streams and endless forests. Now that Ellen was used to the sway of the train, she could open *Anne of Green Gables* and start to read it for the fourth time. The gentle green meadows of Prince Edward Island where

Anne lived seemed more familiar and comfortable than the wilderness outside the train window.

Then the trees thinned out. There were hills and small fields and sometimes a farmhouse made of red brick.

"We're closing in on Toronto," the conductor said. "But it will still be a couple of hours."

By now, everyone in the passenger car was tired and grubby. Children entertained themselves by walking down to the water spigot at the front of the car and coming back up the swaying aisle, balancing paper cups of water. They had run out of games to play and books to read. Then the paper cups ran out.

One question was heard over and over again. "When will we get there?"

Ellen didn't ask this question out loud, but it began going round and round in her mind to the rhythm of the clicking wheels. She leaned her head against Mama's shoulder and fell asleep.

CHAPTER 4

Suddenly Ellen woke and sat up straight. The train was slowing down. Her head was fuzzy with sleep and for a moment she thought that they must be nearly home. But through the dirty window she didn't see dry fields or scattered wooden houses. She saw factories and stores and many houses crowded together, all made of brick.

Then she remembered. This was Toronto. She caught a glimpse down a long street with little houses and stumpy trees. Children were playing on the sidewalks, but before she could really see what they were doing, the train had rolled past.

Moments later, they were under the roof of Union Station, and the train puffed to a stop at the platform. The passengers, who had been sitting still for days, were suddenly in a hurry, pulling their suitcases down, brushing crumbs off skirts and trousers, and making one last try at rubbing away the smears of soot on faces and hands.

Ellen and Mama picked up their two suitcases and waited as patiently as they could in the crowded aisle until it was their turn to jump off the high metal step and onto the platform. Mama immediately started looking for Aunt Gladys.

"I haven't seen her since before you were born," she had said to Ellen back on the train. "But we'll know each other. She looks a lot like my Grandma Lewis. Red hair and light blue eyes. At least, I suppose her hair is still red."

Aunt Gladys's hair was definitely still red. That was the first thing Ellen noticed about her when she came running along the platform calling, "Martha, Martha, Martha! Here I am!" She rushed up to them, put her arms around both of them together, and gave them an enormous hug.

"You're here at last," she said, giving them one more squeeze. "My goodness, little sister, you are skinny. But what did I expect? And this is Ellen! I've waited so long to see you—and look how tall you are! A big girl. But skinny, too. We'll have to feed you up."

She grabbed Ellen's suitcase and herded them along the platform, talking all the time. Ellen lost track of what she was saying as they threaded their way through crowds of people.

They came out into the main hall of the station and stopped for a moment in the middle of a vast space. The arched ceiling was higher than the church steeple at home, Ellen was sure. She craned her neck to see it better. There were birds flying around under that ceiling just as if they were flying under the sky. Ellen thought that if the birds looked down they wouldn't see her at all. They would see only a small speck moving through a crowd of other specks.

They came out of the station and Ellen stopped in her tracks. There were people everywhere, and the street was filled with streetcars clanking and cars and trucks grinding their motors and honking. Across the street was an enormous building with a tall front door and a green roof so high up that Ellen had to tilt her head far back to see it.

Aunt Gladys said proudly, "That's the Royal York Hotel. One of the biggest hotels in the world, they say. Your whole town in Saskatchewan wouldn't fill one floor."

She looked at her watch. "My goodness, I must get home to have supper ready for the boarders at six o'clock sharp. But we'll be there in time. This once we'll take a taxicab. Suitcases are so awkward on the streetcars."

They got into a big black car. Ellen closed her eyes as it started moving. She thought she had seen more people in those first few minutes she had been in Toronto than she had seen in her entire life. She couldn't take in any more.

Then, suddenly, the taxi stopped. Ellen opened her eyes. They were getting out in front of one of the brick houses, a tall one with big windows and an even taller tree growing right in front of it.

Aunt Gladys waved her arm toward the house and said, "That's it. Your new home. I call it Saskatchewan House because I like people to know where I come from. A name makes a boarding house sound respectable, I always think."

She put her hand on Ellen's shoulder. "There are plenty of children living on this street. You won't have any trouble finding friends."

Ellen looked down the street. It seemed to have no end, and it was lined on both sides by one brick house after another. Some were tall but most were small and each one had a porch in front. To Ellen, whose eyes were used to wooden houses painted white or weathered to silver grey, the brick houses looked dark. Even the porches were painted dark red or dark brown. But the late afternoon sun was bright, and some of the houses had a tree and a few flowers growing in front of them.

She turned back toward the taxicab. Aunt Gladys was reaching into her purse and handing the cab driver some coins. Then she picked up Ellen's suitcase and said, "You can meet the kids over there later. I need to get dinner under way."

Kids? For a moment Ellen didn't know what Aunt Gladys was talking about. She looked around in puzzlement and suddenly realized that the porch of the house next door to Saskatchewan House was filled with children. Well, at least six children and they were all staring at Ellen.

Aunt Gladys called out, "You can meet my niece later. I want to get her and her mother settled now."

Ellen was glad to escape from those eyes. She hurried after Aunt Gladys and Mama up the front steps, across the porch, and into Saskatchewan House. After the dazzle of the sunlight, it seemed very dim indoors. Ellen blinked and in a minute she could see that they were standing in a square front hall at the foot of a dark wooden staircase. There was a closed door at the back of the hall and another across from the staircase. Beside the stairs was a window. Ellen peered up at it and saw that it was made of purple and green stained glass. No wonder so little light came through.

Aunt Gladys saw her blinking and said, "I keep the lights switched off in the daytime to save on the electric bill. Your eyes will get used to it. That door at the back goes to the kitchen and the dining room. You'll see those soon enough. The other door used to lead to the parlour, but it's a bedroom now and I've rented it to one of the boarders. This is no time for luxuries like parlours. Now, come on upstairs. You'll be wanting to see your own room."

She led the way up the stairs. They were wide with a carved railing, and they turned halfway up. Ellen thought of the narrow stairs that led to her room in the farmhouse. They were like a ladder compared to this staircase.

On the second floor, there were four more closed doors and a smaller stairway leading to the third floor.

"There are three bedrooms on this floor, plus a bathroom," said Aunt Gladys. "You can take a quick look at the bathroom."

She opened the first door to her left, and Ellen caught a glimpse of a long white bathtub with feet like a lion's and shiny faucets.

Aunt Gladys shut the door and said, "You'll enjoy the tub, I know, but I have to limit you to just four inches of water. You've probably gotten used to bathing in a teacupful so you won't be bothered. There's plenty of water here in Toronto but it costs money to heat it and no one seems to want cold baths, even in summer."

"The other two rooms back here belong to my three girl students. And this room in the front is yours." She pointed with a flourish to the one remaining door. "You two are lucky because a boarder just moved out of this room, and I'm giving it to you. It's the best in the house."

She opened the door and led them through. "Look at this," she said.

Ellen and her mother looked. The room had a bay window looking toward the street, but the big tree Ellen had noticed in front of the house blocked the view and made the light that filled the room cool and a little green. As for the room itself, all Ellen could see was furniture. She had never seen so much furniture in one room. A small table and two chairs stood by the window, and there was a bed along the wall. The rest of the room was filled with more chairs, a large wardrobe and several dressers and cabinets. To the right of the hall door was an archway with a heavy green velvet curtain covering it.

Aunt Gladys went over to look behind the bed. Checking for dust, thought Ellen. She took the chance to whisper to Mama, "There's only one bed."

"And no room for another one," Mama whispered back.

Perhaps Aunt Gladys heard the whispers because she said, "In case you're wondering where you will sleep, Ellen, look behind that curtain."

Ellen reached out to push the curtain aside and found that it was in two parts, like the curtain on the stage in the Sunday School room at home. She pulled one half aside and her eyes opened wide. Behind the curtain was a little room, just big enough for a narrow bed and a small desk with a shelf of books on the wall above it. Beside the desk there was a tall window.

Ellen stepped into the little room and let the curtain close behind her. She went over to the window, hoping she could look past the tree and out on the street, but she couldn't see the street at all. Below the window was the black tarpaper roof of the front porch, and beyond the roof nothing but the tree. She had never seen such a big tree. Its branches and leaves spread before her, and when she stared into them she felt as if she was looking into a new green world.

Mama's voice came from the other room. "Do you like it, sweetie?"

Ellen turned away from the window and took another look around the room. It contained everything she needed. Even the bedspread was her favourite deep blue.

"I love it," she answered and came through the green velvet curtains into the ordinary world of the bigger room.

Mama and Aunt Gladys were pulling out drawers and checking under all the furniture.

"Miss Hinchcliff just left this morning," explained Aunt Gladys. "She is a very tidy person, but you would be surprised at the things people leave behind them. Once I found a live turtle as big as a salad plate, even though I have a strict no-pets rule. I set the turtle free near a pond in the park. Most things people leave are not worth fussing over. But I still check."

Ellen wasn't really listening. She was thinking about the tree.

"What kind of tree is that big one just outside our windows?" she asked. "We don't have any trees half as big on the prairies."

"It's an elm tree," said Aunt Gladys. "And you're right, it's a big one. It's really too close to the house, and it could cause all sorts of problems with its roots breaking the water pipes. But that hasn't happened yet and taking such a big tree down would cost the earth. Anyway, I like the shade. So there it stays."

"I'm glad," said Ellen—and she was. She could imagine

the tree stretching out its branches to shelter her from the strangeness of the street below.

Mama was not so interested in the tree, but she gave Ellen's little room a good inspection. At the end of it, she smiled.

"It's perfect for you," she said. "There's even a light at the end of the bed so you can stay up too late reading and an alarm clock so you won't be late for breakfast. You can sit at the desk and do your lessons once school starts in the fall."

The fall. School. Ellen didn't want to think about those things. Surely by the time school started she would be back on the farm, riding her pony to school. No, she remembered. Star, her pony, had gone with the other animals. It was better to think about the tree.

"I'll leave you to get settled," said Aunt Gladys. "Dinner is at six o'clock sharp. You'll hear the gong. After today, of course, you'll be helping me, Martha, but this is your first night in Toronto. You can both take it easy for a bit. Then we'll have a good meal and you'll meet some of the boarders."

She hurried out leaving Ellen and Mama looking at each other.

"Let's sit here by the window and collect ourselves," said Mama.

Since that was what she always said when too many things were happening all at once, Ellen felt comforted. Some things wouldn't change—even in this house full of strangers in a big strange city.

"This room will be my bedroom and we'll both use it for our sitting room," said Mama. "You'll be close by in your own little room, so you won't be lonely."

Ellen nodded. Somehow she knew that she would be just fine in that room. What made her feel lonely was the thought of the children she had seen next door. She couldn't make friends with so many children at once. In her mind's eye, she saw the long street of brick houses. There would be even more children living in those houses.

There was no way to explain to Mama how strange it made her feel to think of so many children she didn't know. Anyway, Mama had enough things to worry about.

Right now, she was looking at the furniture.

"Miss Hinchcliff must have loved furniture," she said. "We'll need the wardrobe for our clothes, and I'll need one dresser. But that cabinet with glass doors—what on earth would I put in there? I'll ask Gladys to take some of these things away. This room is just too crowded." She looked around one more time.

"These are nice rooms," she decided, "but both of us will have to be neater than we usually are. We're used to a whole house, not just two rooms, so it could be hard. But we have to remember: no clutter."

Ellen laughed. It felt good to laugh. She was imagining

opening her small suitcase and finding it filled with a lot of clutter instead of one dress and a few other bits of clothing. For a while, being neat shouldn't be difficult.

CHAPTER 5

At precisely six o'clock, the sound of a gong echoed through the house, followed by footsteps hurrying down the stairs.

"When Gladys says we eat at six, she means it," said Mama.

She led Ellen down the stairs, through the door at the back of the hall, and into a narrow hallway. On the left was a door that opened to a pantry with shelves from floor to ceiling. Every shelf was crowded with crocks labelled *Flour* and *Sugar,* rows of quart canning jars of red, yellow, and green vegetables and fruits, and cardboard cartons of macaroni and rice.

Mama ran her eyes over it all and said, "We won't go hungry very soon, sweetie." She sighed and Ellen knew she was thinking of the bare kitchen shelves back home.

The next door on the left opened into the kitchen, and right across from it was an archway. Aunt Gladys was just crossing the hall carrying an enormous bowl of potatoes, boiled in their jackets.

"Come on into the dining room," she said. "Most of the boarders are there."

Ellen stepped through the archway and saw a big oval table spread with platters of food. Four women and one man were sitting at the table and she quickly counted five empty chairs. A wide window overlooked a backyard filled by a vegetable garden and a garage at the back.

Aunt Gladys found a place on the table to set the potatoes among platters of cold ham, sliced tomatoes, cabbage slaw, bread, and pickles. Suddenly, Ellen was very hungry.

Her aunt pointed to the chair nearest the kitchen. "That's where I sit and you can sit there on my right, Martha, so we both can jump up and fetch things easily. You can sit next to your ma, Ellen. I'll introduce you to everyone as soon as we get some food on our plates."

She plumped herself down, bowed her head, and said very quickly, "For what we are about to receive, the Lord make us truly thankful."

She raised her head, looked around the table, and added, "In these hard times, it's right for us to be thankful that we are well fed. Now, let's pass the serving dishes."

For a few minutes, Ellen was busy helping herself to some of everything. She couldn't remember when she had seen such food. Maybe when she was a very little girl.

After a few delicious bites, she took a deep breath and looked around the table. She was mortified to see that everyone was looking at her.

Aunt Gladys said, "It's a pleasure to us all to see you enjoy your dinner so much, child. Now, let me introduce everyone."

Ellen looked down at her plate. Suddenly, she had no appetite at all. What would these people think of her? A rude girl from the prairies. That's what they would think.

Mama cleared her throat and said, "Ellen, Aunt Gladys is speaking to you."

"Yes, I am," said Aunt Gladys. "We all share this house so it's important that we know each other. Ellen, on your right is Miss Sprucedale. She works downtown at Eaton's Department Store. In the millinery department. That's hats, dear. Miss Sprucedale has the parlour room. She's very good with a needle and saves me a pretty penny with her mending."

Miss Sprucedale had golden hair in tight curls all over her head, and she looked what Mama called *youthful*—though Ellen, sitting right next to her, could see that the powder on her face had settled into the wrinkles around her eyes.

She smiled at Ellen and said, "It will be so nice having a girl like you in the house. And Martha, I can always let you know when we have a good sale happening at Eaton's."

Aunt Gladys was going on. "The three along the side there all live on the second floor with you, and they are all students at the university. Addy and Bertha share the big room, and Caroline has the little one. A, B, and C, I call them. You'll have to fight with them to get into the bathroom in the morning."

All three girls nodded at Ellen and Mama and said

"How do you do?" very quickly and all together. Then they looked at each other and laughed. Ellen had to smile back. She stopped feeling so uncomfortable.

"We only have one representative of the third floor with us today," Aunt Gladys said. "Mr. Martineau is now a streetcar driver, but he is also a lawyer and gives me good advice when I'm dealing with the city." She shook her head. "It's not always easy carrying on a business and it's very reassuring to have Mr. Martineau on my side."

Mr. Martineau nodded pleasantly, but he didn't smile or say anything. He was very thin and had bright black eyes that looked out from beneath heavy grey eyebrows. Ellen thought that he looked sad.

"The two empty chairs belong to the Third Floor Boys. They're brothers and they work down on the waterfront, but when they have a day or two off, they go out to the country to help their parents on their little farm along the lake. They came from Italy, and that family is coping with this Depression better than most people. They grow plenty for themselves, and there's enough for the boys to pay their rent in vegetables and fruit. Not to mention eggs. That's a blessing to all of us. It's why we can eat so well." She gestured at the platters on the table which were being rapidly emptied.

Aunt Gladys went into the kitchen and came back with an enormous teapot. Miss Sprucedale and the ABC girls poured tea for themselves, but Mr. Martineau excused himself and left.

"He's a very quiet man," Aunt Gladys said, once he had gone. "He was a successful lawyer but he bought too many houses and couldn't keep up the payments. The bank took them all and he didn't have enough money to keep his law office going. I think he kind of gave up. Now he's lucky to be driving a streetcar. It pays his rent but I think, deep down, he misses being a lawyer."

When the tea was gone, Addie, Bertha, and Caroline rapidly cleared the table. Ellen could hear them in the kitchen, washing dishes and chattering.

"Are there classes in the summer?" Mama asked. "I would have thought they would go home for their vacation."

"They have to work like everyone else," said Aunt Gladys. "There's no work where they come from and they were lucky to get summer jobs cleaning hotel rooms downtown."

"I'll get a job, too," said Mama. "And, of course I'll help with the housework. So will Ellen. We don't want to be a burden on you."

"You won't be a burden," said Aunt Gladys. "I did all my calculations before I sent you that letter, and I promise you won't send me into bankruptcy. I own this house free and clear, and I run a tight ship and don't waste anything. The boys' farm stuff helps and so does the garden out back. And everybody helps a bit with the work of the house. That's what I tell them when they rent a room. Clean your own room, I say, and take on some job to help us all. And they all do. You'll be helping me in the morning and with the housekeeping in general."

She looked at Ellen. "As for you, I'm thinking of getting some chickens. If I do, I'll give you the job of looking after them. I expect that you know something about chickens."

Ellen jumped. She had almost stopped listening but luckily the word *chickens* had caught her ear, so she could say, "I feed the chickens at home, Aunt Gladys, and I'd be glad to do it here, too."

Mama looked at her and said, "Why don't you go up and unpack and get settled in your room, Ellen? We've come a long way in the last few days. I'll have a visit with Gladys and be up in a little while."

Ellen was grateful. She couldn't put chickens and this brick house with its dark wood and stained-glass windows together in her mind. It just didn't make sense. There was no room here for chickens. They would need a chicken yard, wouldn't they?

She remembered her manners and said, "Thank you for the wonderful dinner." She also remembered how to get from the dining room to the stairs and which door to open on the second floor.

Mama's room with all its furniture looked unfriendly, as if it was expecting more people to arrive and sit in its chairs. Without pausing, Ellen parted the green velvet curtain and entered her own small room. Instantly, it seemed to fold around her and welcome her. The cream-coloured walls, the deep blue bedspread, and the green curtain over the archway were restful, and outside the window the green leaves of the elm tree stirred gently in the light wind.

CHAPTER 6

Ellen opened her suitcase. She shook out her red-and-white dress and hung it in the wardrobe in Mama's room. Then she took her other clothes out of the suitcase and put them neatly in the middle drawer of the desk.

If I ever get more clothes, I have two empty drawers to put them in, she thought as she lined up her dress-up shoes under the bed and put on her more comfortable brown pair.

The desk had a slanted front that opened down to form the writing surface. Inside were little cubbyholes to hold envelopes and cards and pencils, all empty. In the centre of the cubbyholes was a small drawer. Ellen opened it, sure that it would be empty, too. But it wasn't.

Lying in the drawer was a little notebook with a shiny cover like a green-and-black checkerboard. Ellen took it from the drawer. It just covered her hand and felt smooth.

She opened the notebook and saw that the pages were lined. At the top of the first page, someone had printed in neat letters: PLANS. That was all. Every other page was blank.

For a moment Ellen thought that Miss Hinchcliff must have forgotten the notebook, but then she shook her head.

Miss Hinchcliff had not left one thing in all the drawers and shelves in Mama's room. She wouldn't start a notebook and then forget about it.

The notebook must have belonged to someone else, thought Ellen. Someone who had no plans, so she'd left it behind. No plans—just like me.

She closed the notebook. "You'll have to wait for someone with plans," she told it and put it back into the drawer and shut the desk.

There was still one thing missing. Ellen went into Mama's room and chose one of the straight chairs. It fit perfectly in front of the desk.

She looked around the room. It was tidy and comfortable. She glanced at the books on the shelf above the desk. They all looked as if they had been read many times. There was her old friend, *Anne of Green Gables,* and another favourite, *Little Women*.

Her hand went to a thick red book called *The Secret Garden*. She took it down and put it on her bed. A book to read before she went to sleep. A book about a secret.

The books reminded Ellen that she had not unpacked her book bag. She took out her copy of *Anne of Green Gables* and put it next to the one on the shelf. She stuck the pencils and sharpener and her scribbler into the cubbyholes in the desk. Then she took out the two one-dollar bills her father had sent and put them into the little drawer, under the green-and-black notebook.

Nice and safe, she thought. Now what can I do? I can't go downstairs and interrupt Mama. I'd just have to listen to her and Aunt Gladys talk. And Aunt Gladys would say I should go out and meet the kids on the street.

The very thought made her stomach clench up. All those eyes staring at her and her too-short dress and her Saskatchewan ways. If only the kids weren't there, she could take a walk down the street and look at the houses.

But the kids *were* there. She could hear their voices coming up from the street, though she couldn't make out what they were saying. She got up from the bed where she was sitting and went to the window.

The voices were a little clearer now. They were calling something. It sounded like "ally-ally-in-free." She knew those words. They meant the kids were playing hide-and-seek or some game like that.

She pressed her nose against the window, wishing she could at least catch a glimpse of the children, but it was no use. The tree blocked her view of the street.

She looked down. There was the roof of the front porch outside the window. It was flat and looked very solid. She stepped back to look at the tall window. It reached down almost to the floor and had a latch at one side.

Ellen reached out and turned the handle. She tugged gently and the window opened like a door. There was no screen. Without pausing for a moment, she stepped over the windowsill and onto the porch roof. The bay window of Mama's room was to her left, and to her right she could see the porch roof of the house next door. That was all.

In front of her, the leaves of the tree were like a thick screen, hiding the street below. She took a step and then another. Now she was closer to the tree. And close to the edge of the porch roof. Looking down she could see the front steps of Saskatchewan House and the bottom steps of the house next door.

Ellen suddenly remembered standing in the opening of the barn loft on the farm while Adam, the boy who lived up the road, dared her to jump. She had finally done it—but this roof was definitely higher than the barn loft, and landing on the steps below would be a bad idea. She decided to step back from the edge.

She moved back until she could feel the solid wood of the window frame behind her. Maybe she should just go back to the safety of her room.

No, she didn't want to go back. Not yet.

She listened to the voices from the street again. They were louder now. "Because I'm outside," she said to herself. "I'm outside but they can't see me. They don't even know I'm here."

She smiled to herself. It was like being invisible. She could hear the children down on the ground, but they had no idea she was listening.

Some voice inside her whispered, "Sneaky."

Ellen answered the voice. "They're yelling. Anyone can hear them."

The voice stopped whispering but the word *sneaky* stayed in Ellen's mind like an echo.

She ignored it. She could tell now that the children in the street were playing hide-and-seek, just as she had thought. There seemed to be a little girl who had a hard time finding good hiding places. She kept begging for help from another girl named Charlene.

"Help me, Charlene. I don't want Joey to find me. *Please,* Charlene."

An older voice answered, "I'll help you this time, Gracie, but you have to learn to find your own places. Come on. Joey's counting. We have to run."

Ellen listened, fascinated. She could imagine Charlene, a tall girl about eleven years old with long blonde braids down her back. And Gracie would be her little sister. And Joey, their brother who was counting rapidly to one hundred, would be short and able to run very fast.

The next thing she heard was Joey saying, "Ha! I knew Charlene would push you under the porch. Got ya, Gracie."

Gracie cried but Charlene said, "Don't give him the satisfaction, Gracie. He just likes to be mean. Here, take this chalk and draw on the sidewalk."

After that, the voices grew quieter and Ellen could only hear a word or two. She wished she could see the children, but even if she went to the edge of the roof, the tree would be in the way.

Just then she heard sounds from inside the house. A door opened and Mama's voice was calling her. Quickly, Ellen stepped over the windowsill and back into the room. She shut the window and was sitting on her bed when her mother pushed aside the curtain.

"You look excited," she said. "Did something happen?"

"Not really," said Ellen. "I guess I'm just surprised to have such a perfect room. And I'm all unpacked. I even have two empty drawers so there will be no clutter."

To herself she said, "It's true. Nothing *did* happen. And if we were at home on the farm, Mama wouldn't even ask me if something happened. It's just because we are in a strange place."

Mama sat down beside Ellen. "I hope you're going to be happy here," she said. "I'm going to be pretty busy, I can tell, and you'll be on your own a lot. Of course, that's not so different from your life on the farm. But this is all strange to you." She waved her arm to take in the room and the street and the city beyond. "It will be easier when you make some friends."

Ellen remembered the voices. Charlene. Maybe she could be a friend. Later.

"I'll try," she said. She pointed to *The Secret Garden*. "Until I do, I have some books to read."

"I expect you'll do fine, sweetie," said Mama. She yawned. "I think it's time for both of us to go to bed. Remember, we just got off the train this afternoon."

Ellen suddenly realized she *was* very tired. It was getting dark and she could no longer hear the children's voices. They must have gone into their houses.

She took *The Secret Garden* to bed with her but fell asleep before she could even open it. It was Mama who turned out the light.

CHAPTER 7

The next morning, Ellen was wakened by light that filled her room. She opened her eyes, blinked, and closed them tight. Then she slowly opened them again and looked around. Her room at home had small windows under the eaves and a ceiling that slanted over her bed. It was cozy but always a little dim. This ceiling was high over her head and the big window let in a flood of early morning sun, shining through the leaves of the tree.

Mama stuck her head through the opening in the curtain.

"Good, you're awake," she said. "Breakfast starts in fifteen minutes. If we hurry we won't be late."

Ellen pulled on her clothes and went out into the hall to try her luck at getting into the bathroom. Addie was already waiting outside the door. She smiled and said, "It's no fun to wait but we sure didn't have anything like this bathroom up in the Ottawa Valley where I come from. It was the outhouse and then a tin basin for washing up."

"I know," said Ellen. "It's just like that on the farm. What I really love here is the bathtub with its claw feet like a lion. If there was ever enough hot water, I could lie down and float in that bathtub. It's so big."

"Well, there never will be enough hot water," said Addie, "but the tub is still wonderful." Just then the door opened and she darted in. "I'll be quick," she said.

Breakfast was a very quiet and efficient meal of smooth oatmeal with plenty of milk, toast, and tea. Everyone had to get to work so they didn't waste time talking. The only one who stayed to drink an extra cup of tea was Mr. Martineau.

"I'm working the afternoon shift, so I have time to read all the bad news," he said and disappeared behind the newspaper.

When the ABC girls and Miss Sprucedale had left, Ellen helped Aunt Gladys and Mama clear up the breakfast dishes.

Then Aunt Gladys said, "Why don't you go and play outside, Ellen? I'm going to give Martha a tour of the pantry and the kitchen cupboards and you don't need to go through all that."

Ellen thought fast. "I want to write a letter to my friend Sarah and tell her about Saskatchewan House. I have some paper in my scribbler but I'll need an envelope."

"I have plenty of envelopes," said Aunt Gladys. "You're welcome to them any time. And I have some stamps, too."

"Thank you, Aunt Gladys," said Ellen. She was almost out the door when she remembered the notebook. "I forgot to tell you—I found a little notebook in the desk. It's kind of pretty and it's mostly blank. Do you think it belongs to Miss Hinchcliff?"

"I wouldn't think so," said Aunt Gladys. "She never used the desk. It probably belonged to a young woman, Eliza something-or-other, who had the room for a few weeks. She was all set to start a job in an office downtown but her mother got sick and Eliza had to go home. I don't know where she is now. Consider the notebook yours."

"Thanks," said Ellen. She ran upstairs thinking about Eliza who had never had time to write down her plans. "Maybe I will have some plans to write down someday," she told herself. "I'm sure Eliza wouldn't mind."

Right now she was glad to avoid the children next door and write a letter to Sarah whom she suddenly missed very much.

She took her scribbler from the desk, carefully tore out two pages, and started to write as neatly as she could.

Dear Sarah,

Here I am in Saskatchewan House. That's what Aunt Gladys calls her boarding house. It's much bigger than any house I've ever seen and has more people living in it, too. Besides me and Mama and Aunt G. there are three college girls, one lady who works at Eaton's, one man who drives a streetcar, and two I haven't met yet. Aunt G. calls them boys but I think they are men.

So that's a lot of people and there's lots of food and furniture. Aunt G. says there are some kids living near Saskatchewan House but I don't know how to meet them. Or maybe I don't want to. I wish you were next door instead. Everyone says, "Go out and play." But that is hard. I think you will know what I mean.

I wish I could send you a ham sandwich or a jar of peaches.

Love,

Ellen

Ellen folded the letter and put it on top of the desk so that she would see it and remember to get an envelope and mail it. Then she sat on her bed and thought about what to do next. She couldn't hear any voices out on the street. Maybe all the children were away. Maybe it would be safe to go out on the porch.

She went slowly downstairs and out the front door, closing it gently behind her, and walked very quietly to the top of the porch steps. She didn't want to attract any attention.

There were no children in sight but she could see a ball lying in the gutter and chalk markings on the sidewalk, so she knew they had been playing there not long ago. Maybe yesterday.

She went down the steps to the sidewalk and looked at the house next door. It was much smaller than Saskatchewan House. It had two stories instead of three and it was just wide enough for a window beside the front door and one bay window in the room above the porch.

Charlene and Joey and Gracie must live there, she thought. And their parents. That's enough for such a small house.

She stared at the little house trying to imagine what she might say to Charlene if she just happened to come out right now. But it was a boy who suddenly burst out of the front door, leapt over the porch railing, and landed with a crash. He saw Ellen standing on the sidewalk and let out a whoop. He rushed over to her, thumped her on the arm, yelled, "You're it!" and dashed away down the street.

Ellen was so startled she couldn't say a word. Her one thought was to bolt up the steps of Saskatchewan House, and get back to her room. She was halfway across the porch when she heard the boy say, "Hey!"

She had to stop and turn around. He couldn't think she was running away—even if she was. He stood at the bottom of the steps with his arms crossed and stared up at her. His eyes were round and black, and his hair was black, too. Ellen had never seen such black hair.

After a minute the boy said, "Hey Saskatchewan, don't you even know how to play tag?"

When Ellen didn't answer he shook his head in disgust and walked away down the street with his hands in the pockets of his short pants.

Ellen went into the house and straight up to her room. That was Joey. I know it was. And he'll tell Charlene that I'm a stupid girl from a farm. Doesn't know anything! she thought miserably as she sat on the bed.

After a few minutes she began to get mad. "He didn't even say hello. He just yelled at me. It's not fair. Now Charlene will think that I'm stupid and she'll never want to speak to me. Of course I don't want to talk to her anyway."

She unfolded the letter to Sarah, picked up her pencil and wrote,

PS. Now I have met one of the kids next door and I don't think I will ever want to play with them. Oh, I do wish you were here.

As she was refolding the letter she heard her mother come into the big room. She waited, but Mama didn't part the curtain and speak to her. For a few minutes she moved around the room and then Ellen heard her sit down in one of the chairs.

"Mama," she called. "Are you there?"

"Yes, I'm just sitting here thinking. I thought you were probably outside."

"I was," said Ellen. "But there were no kids to play with so I came in."

"Well, come on in here and I'll tell you what I'm thinking about."

Ellen found her mother sitting at the table in the bay window so she went and sat in the other chair. Her mother smiled at her.

"I've learned a lot about how this house runs. It's different from the farm but I can be a big help to Gladys. She's being very good to us, giving us these nice rooms and all. But I know that if I don't get a job and start putting some money into the household, she'll get a little edgy. She really does need money coming in. I want to pay some of our room and board in cash so that she won't feel that she's giving too much."

She stopped for a minute and then went on. "If I can get a job it will mean that you'll have to do some of my kitchen chores. It all depends on what job I get. If I can get one at all."

"I can't do everything you can do, but if it's clearing the table and washing the dishes I can do that," said Ellen. She didn't know what it would be like to work for Aunt Gladys. She might be very fussy. But working for Aunt Gladys would probably be easier than making friends with the children next door. Maybe she would be so busy that she wouldn't even have time for them.

"I'll try, Mama," she said. "I'll really try."

CHAPTER 8

It didn't take long for Mama to find a job.

"Toronto's not so different from a small town in Saskatchewan," she told Ellen. "You have to put out the word if you want to buy a cow or get a job. If you're lucky someone who has a cow to sell or a job for you will hear the news, and you might get just what you want."

Mama's job came about because Aunt Gladys happened to have a conversation with a woman who ran a bakery down on Bloor Street.

"She says that one of my old neighbours is living up near Casa Loma," Aunt Gladys told Mama and Ellen. "You know Casa Loma, don't you?"

They shook their heads so she went on, "There was a rich man years ago who wanted to have a castle of his own. So he built Casa Loma. It's a big house with a grand hall and towers and a high wall all around it. But the man wasn't rich enough and he ran out of money, and now his castle stands there, empty, with its walls and its towers going to rack and ruin. You can see it up on the hill when you walk up Bathurst Street."

"Anyway, this woman is all alone in her big fancy house not far from Casa Loma and she's getting old. She needs someone to come in and do housekeeping in the mornings. I haven't seen her in years but if you tell her you are my sister she might just hire you. Her name is Mrs. Bartholomew now but her name used to be Mrs. Biggins, so I just call her Mrs. B."

Mama went the very next day to see Mrs. B. and came home with a job.

"She does need help with the house," she said to Ellen. "But I think she hired me because I listened. She spent an hour telling me all about her husband and how he died. She's lonely."

"And she wants you to come every day?"

"Every morning but Sunday. On Sunday her daughter takes her to church. I'll have plenty to do. The house is enormous and she wants it all to be kept very clean, even though she only uses a few rooms on the first floor and her bedroom upstairs. So I'll be mopping marble floors and polishing the mahogany banister. And picking dead leaves off the floor of the plant room. Mrs. B. has dozens of plants."

"Is the house beautiful?" asked Ellen.

"It's too grand for me," said Mama. "And everything in it is black or grey or white. Mrs. B. doesn't like colour."

"What about the plants?" asked Ellen. "There must be flowers."

"No flowers," said Mama. "Fortunately, the plants are allowed to be green. I'll be wearing a grey apron trimmed in white lace, but I do have a job. Thank goodness. And that means that you have a job, too. I'll have to leave the minute I finish breakfast, so you'll be the one to help your aunt with the clearing up. And you'll have to fix lunch for yourself. Gladys doesn't prepare lunch for anyone. I'll be home in plenty of time to do my share at dinnertime. You'll have to look after yourself most of the day. Can I count on you to take care of all that?"

"Of course," said Ellen, but she wondered what she would do all day long. She didn't ask because she knew that Mama would say, "You can always go play with the children next door."

On the first day of her job, Mama was up at six. Before she went downstairs to stir oatmeal and set the table, she stuck her head through the curtain and said, "See you in ten minutes, Sunshine."

Ellen never felt like sunshine in the morning but she couldn't let Mama down, so she sat up, put her feet on the floor, and hoped that no one would be in the bathroom so early in the morning. She looked forward to taking a little extra time to enjoy the warm water flowing over her hands while she made faces in the mirror with the gold-painted frame. Luckily, the ABC girls weren't up yet and the bathroom was all Ellen's.

By eight o'clock Mama had set off to walk over to Bathurst Street and up the steep hill to the neighbourhood of big houses. A few minutes later, the ABC girls and Miss Sprucedale were on their way to their jobs downtown. Mr. Martineau took the newspaper out to the front porch to read. No one was left in Saskatchewan House but Ellen and Aunt Gladys.

The two of them worked together clearing the table and then Aunt Gladys washed the dishes and Ellen dried. Ellen was surprised that her talkative aunt didn't chat while she swished silverware in the soapy water.

As Ellen dried the spoons, Aunt Gladys seemed to read her thoughts. "I guess you've noticed how quiet I am in the mornings. Well, I've learned that it takes me at least three hours to really wake up. I can get my work done without thinking about it, but I can't talk at the same time. I trust that you don't mind."

Ellen smiled at her aunt. "I don't mind," she said.

In fact, far from minding, Ellen was glad. Back home she was used to eating breakfast alone because her father and mother were usually busy in the barn or the fields while she got ready for school. They would come in and sit down for a cup of tea with her just before she set off. Eating breakfast with eight or nine other people was quite a change, even if they were quiet.

Aunt Gladys rinsed out the sink and hung up the dishcloth.

She turned to Ellen and said, "Now I'll go downstairs and have some time to myself. You can do whatever you like as long as you don't leave Manning Avenue. I'm not going to search the city for you. Go out and play with the children on the street. That will keep you busy. And don't come bothering me. My quarters are off limits."

Three mornings passed and Ellen did not leave Manning Avenue and she did not bother Aunt Gladys. But she did not go out to the street to meet the children. Instead, she read *The Secret Garden* from cover to cover. Mary, the girl in the book, also found herself living in a place she did not know at all. Ellen shivered when she thought of the vast and nearly empty house Mary had to live in. No cozy little room and mother nearby for Mary. But Mary only had to get to know two other children, not a whole crowd who already had their games and their familiar fights.

On the fourth morning of Mama's job, Ellen went up to her room as usual. But today she had nothing to do. She didn't want to read another book. Her room was tidy. She had no more to tell Sarah, so there was no point in writing a letter.

She stood at the open window. No breeze blew in. The leaves of the tree weren't moving at all. It was going to be a hot, still day. A hot, still, boring day.

Suddenly she heard a voice from down the street. It shouted, "You're it!"

She knew that voice. It was Joey for sure. He sounded just the way he did when he tagged her. The memory made her both mad and ashamed all over again. Why couldn't she have thought of something smart to say?

She heard more voices now. What were they talking about? But the words were lost.

There was only one thing to do. Ellen stepped over the windowsill. It would be easy to sit down, lean against the house, and listen.

For a moment she stood by the window, but she could still hear only a few words now and then, usually when somebody shouted, "I won't be It again," or "You always go too fast," and she wasn't sure who the voices belonged to. A breeze had come up and the leaves on the tree were rustling.

"This is no good. I need to get where I can see," Ellen decided. She looked around more carefully than she had before. At one end of the roof was the slanted side of the bay window in Mama's room. In front of that window rose the trunk of the big tree, smooth and grey. A branch came out from the trunk, just above the edge of the porch roof.

Ellen walked over to see it better. It was a big branch.

About as big around as Star, my pony, thought Ellen. If I could get my legs around it, I could sit on it just like I used to sit on Star.

She looked closely at the branch. It nearly touched the corner of the roof and then slanted away toward the street, quite level until about halfway across the yard where it forked into two smaller branches that turned up quite sharply.

She looked back at the place where the branch was right beside the edge of the roof.

"It would be easy to swing my leg over and sit on it," Ellen said to herself, "Then I could scoot myself along." A memory flashed into her mind. She was sitting on the big rafter in the barn loft. A bird had built a nest on the rafter and abandoned it after the baby birds flew away. Ellen wanted to take it to school and Dad said that if she could get it, she could have it.

She could remember Dad below her, looking up and saying, "Just go slow. I'll be here to catch you if you fall."

Well, he wasn't here now, but at least the branch didn't have corners like the beam. It would be easier to sit on.

I only have to get out to where it forks, Ellen convinced herself. Then I'll be able to see down into the street.

Before she could think any more, she was sitting astride the branch, too busy moving herself along to be scared. The tree seemed to be holding her. It was not moving at all.

She inched along looking down at her hands, firm on the gray bark, as she moved toward the place where the branch divided. It seemed to take a very long time, and when she got there she felt as if she had come on a long journey.

She looked ahead of her and saw that she had reached the end of this particular journey. There was no way she could move any farther. But there was another small branch beside her, just where she could reach it and hold on. She forgot about the children who might be below her and looked around at the inside world of the tree.

It was a green world. She was surrounded by a maze of branches and a canopy of leaves. She could glimpse the sky and the red brick of the house across the street but only in bits that changed as the leaves moved gently. When she turned her head she could see the roof she had come from, not so far away.

Ellen took a deep breath. She felt like an explorer who had set out looking for a city and had found a deep forest instead. For a few moments she sat quietly, feeling the strength of the tree and resting her eyes on the green.

Then she heard a sharp voice shout right beneath her.

"Joey, come out of there this minute!"

It was Charlene's voice. For the first time Ellen looked down. She couldn't see very much. The tree had some small lower branches that got in the way but she could catch a glimpse of Charlene's red dress and the top of her head. Her hair was dark brown and wavy, not blonde. She must be standing on the sidewalk. But where was Joey?

A door slammed and Ellen heard loud footsteps crossing

a wooden porch. Charlene said, "You know that Mum doesn't want us in the house while she's at work."

She wasn't shouting now but Ellen could hear her clearly.

Good, she thought. And I'm safe as long as they don't look up.

"But I'm hungry," said Joey. "I just wanted to get some bread and jelly."

Now Charlene sounded more sad than cross. "You especially can't sneak food. What if Mum comes home and there's not enough bread for supper? She left sandwiches for lunch and I hid them until then where you'll never find them. So go and play. But don't go up to the castle. You know you have to stay where you can hear me."

Joey didn't answer. Ellen could hear him running off down the street and the shouts of boys greeting him as he ran.

The castle, she thought. It must be that Casa Loma Aunt Gladys told us about. What would Joey be doing at an abandoned castle?

Below her, she heard Charlene say, "Come on Gracie. Let's go down the street and play hopscotch with Pearl."

Then the voices were gone. Ellen stretched one arm out and then the other. She felt stiff from listening so hard. Suddenly a new sound made her jump. Someone was walking across the porch of Saskatchewan House and opening the front door.

Oh no, thought Ellen. That must be Mama back from work. She's early.

For a moment she couldn't move, but the thought of having to explain made her brave. By holding on to the small branch beside her she managed to turn around. The roof was closer than she thought, but it still took her several minutes to scoot along until she could put her feet safely on the tarpaper and take the few quick steps to the open window and over the sill.

Ellen gently closed the window behind her and listened. She couldn't hear footsteps on the stairs or the creak of the door to Mama's room opening. She took a deep breath and sat down on the bed and waited.

CHAPTER 9

The Secret Garden was lying beside Ellen on the bed. She opened it somewhere in the middle but she didn't see what was written there. Would Mama believe that she had chosen to stay indoors on a beautiful day and reread a book she had just finished?

"I have to tell her that I can't make friends so fast," she said out loud.

She heard the door open. Then the curtains parted and her mother came into the little room.

She was smiling, not at Ellen, but at a paper she was holding in her hand.

"Oh, you *are* here," she said. "I called you from the bottom of the stairs. Didn't you hear me? I thought you must have gone out to play with those children."

"No," said Ellen. "I was just here, thinking. Has something happened? You look very happy."

"I *am* happy," said Mama, "and I have two surprises for you."

She sat down on the bed beside Ellen and gave her a hug. "The best one is that we got a letter from your dad.

That's why it took me so long to come up. I had to read enough to be sure he's all right. And he is. That's what's making me happy."

"But he doesn't know we're here," said Ellen. "How did he send us a letter?"

"It must have come just after we left the farm and Jack sent it on right away. It followed us here. But now we know where Mike is and we can write and tell him all about what we're doing. He's in Alberta, Ellen. Here, you can read what he says."

Ellen read:

Dear Girls,

I'm up in the Peace River country. They haven't had a crop failure here and I can get enough farm work to keep going and earn a little money to send to you. I'm boarding at a farmhouse and the food isn't bad but not as good as what you cook, Martha. Ellen, I hope you are helping your mama as much as you can. In these hard times we need each other. I wish I was with you but this is the best I can do now. Two of the dollars I'm sending are for you. Do something good with them.

He went on to talk about the Saskatchewan farm, and Mama took the letter back from Ellen.

"We'll both sleep better knowing that he isn't wandering

the country," she said. "There are so many men out there going from place to place, looking for work. Begging for food sometimes. But Mike has work and shelter. And so do we. And even a little extra now and then."

She took two one-dollar bills from the envelope and handed them to Ellen.

"Do you have a good place to keep them?" she asked.

"A perfect place," said Ellen.

She went to the desk and put the bills into the little drawer with the others her dad had sent. Now she had four dollars. Enough to buy something important.

Her mother was reading the letter again, but she looked up and smiled. "I said two surprises, remember? This letter is the best one but the other is nice, too. Mrs. B. has given me some dresses that her granddaughter has outgrown. They're almost your size. Much better than those skimpy ones we brought from Saskatchewan. We'll just have to shorten them a little."

She got up and parted the green curtains.

"Come in here where the mirror is," she said, opening the wardrobe door. There was a mirror inside and looking at her reflection Ellen could see that her red-and-white checked dress was faded and short. She could also see a few scrapes on the inside of her knees where she had been gripping the branch of the tree so tightly. She'd have to keep her mother from seeing those scrapes.

Mama was taking a stack of dresses out of a big bag. More than will fit into my suitcase when we go back to Saskatchewan, Ellen thought. Then she was swept up in the fun of trying on a blue dress with white buttons shaped like tulips up the front, and a yellow-and-white striped sundress, and more.

Some were far too big, but in the end Ellen had four new dresses that needed to be shortened but otherwise fit perfectly.

"We'll keep the bigger ones for you to grow into," said Mama. "I think Mrs. B.'s granddaughter must have a very large wardrobe. These are hardly worn. You like the blue one best, don't you? I can shorten it after lunch and you can wear it to dinner. I think we should turn your old checked one into a dust cloth. It's too worn to pass on to anyone."

At the table that night Miss Sprucedale took special notice of Ellen's new dress. "It's just what all the girls are wearing," she said.

Aunt Gladys shook her head. "What the ones who can *afford* it are wearing," she said. "You see fashion there at the store, Miss Sprucedale, but there are many who won't even go in because they can't buy anything. Ellen is lucky that Mrs. B. is so generous."

Just for a moment Ellen wished she could have walked into Eaton's and chosen this very dress for herself. Nevertheless, after dinner she wrote Mrs. B. a thank-you note.

Dear Mrs. Bartholomew,

You were so kind to send me the lovely dresses. Please tell your granddaughter I like them very much.

Yours truly,

Ellen Jackson

"That's very nice, Ellen," said Mama. "I'll take it to her in the morning. I've told her all about you and how you're having to get used to living in the city. Which reminds me, are you getting to know the children next door?"

"A little," said Ellen. "The big girl is Charlene and she has a brother and a sister. She's very busy looking after them."

It's all true, she thought. I just haven't met them in person. And Mama just wants to know that I'm settling in.

But the voice in her head that said *sneaky* was ready to speak up so she added, out loud. "I have to think of things to do by myself a lot of the time."

"As long as you're not too bored," said Mama. "I don't want Gladys to feel she has to entertain you after you help her tidy up in the mornings. After her work is done she likes her time alone in her rooms in the basement. Her 'hidey-hole,' I call it. I haven't even been down there myself. Can I count on you to look after yourself and not do anything foolish?"

Ellen didn't want to think about whether Mama would say that going out on the tree branch was foolish. After all, she must know how she and Adam and Sarah climbed around in the barn. This was not so different.

She said, "I'll look after myself, Mama, and I won't go away from the house."

She was glad to think that the last part was certainly true. Being up in the tree was practically the same as being in the house. The tree was the special, secret part of her room. It was like the secret garden in the book she had just read. A place no one else knew about. She could hardly wait till the next time she could be there.

CHAPTER 10

Mornings in Saskatchewan House were always exactly the same. Once the breakfast dishes were done, the house was quiet. Aunt Gladys was in her basement hidey-hole and everyone else was off at work. If Mr. Martineau was working a late shift, he might be sitting on the front porch reading the newspaper. He never paid any attention to what Ellen was doing.

So Ellen was alone. But she didn't mind being alone because the tree was waiting. She always spent exactly ten minutes tidying her room before she opened the window, just in case Mama forgot something and came back and found her, not in her room, not playing with the kids next door, but up in a tree, listening and watching.

As she made her bed and tidied her room, Ellen tried to think of explaining the tree to her mother. Why she loved being out on the branch, surrounded by leaves. Why she was listening. Why she wanted to know the neighbours before she had to meet them and talk to them.

Mama might say she was eavesdropping. Or spying. Or she would start to worry that Ellen was not happy.

When Ellen looked at the clock and saw the ten minutes had passed, she could be quite sure that her mother was safely gone for the morning. The problem of telling her about the tree could wait for another day.

It was time to open the window, and step over the window-sill. In three steps she would be sitting on the thick branch, ready to hear a little more from the neighbourhood below.

As she sat in the listening tree, Ellen was learning some things about the children who played and talked and argued below her.

Charlene was two years older than Joey, who didn't stay around too much. He was always running off to play in the laneways with other boys.

"Just tell me where you're going!" Charlene shouted at him today, just as she did every day. "You know that's my job. I have to know where you are. That's what Mum says."

"I did tell you!" Joey shouted back. "But you never listen."

Ellen thought she was the only person who knew that they were both telling the truth. Joey usually called out something as he ran off down the street, but he seemed to be able to choose a moment when Charlene was too busy to hear him.

Today he was late for lunch and Charlene said, "You've been up at the castle again, haven't you? You know that's off limits. The police might even catch you."

"Not likely," Joey said. "Nobody cares about the castle now. There are plenty of places to hide and there are so many stones missing from the wall that we can get away easy. Anyway we're just playing."

Charlene sighed so loudly that Ellen could hear her. "Just never, *never* let Mum know," she said. "She would say I was responsible. But how can I be responsible for a kid like you, especially when I have to look after Gracie, too? It's not fair."

She sighed again and Ellen understood that Charlene was jealous. Joey could do the wrong thing and play up at the mysterious castle, but Charlene had to stay home and be responsible.

I'm more like Joey, she thought. I'm only responsible for drying dishes. And then I'm up in this tree, listening. Maybe it's the wrong thing to do but I'm not going to stop. Just like Joey.

Down below Joey said, "Well, now I'm going into the laneway to ride Brian's bike. Honest."

Ellen knew he was grinning as he ran off. She turned her attention to the girls. They always played in front of the houses.

The girls were Charlene, Gracie, Pearl, and Jeanette. Gracie, Charlene's little sister, was four years old and wanted someone to play with her all the time.

"Gracie, honey," Charlene said now, "I can't play dolls

for one more minute. Come and skip rope with Pearl and Jeanette and me."

"You go too fast," Gracie whined. "You trip me up on purpose."

"We don't," said Charlene. "You just have to learn to skip faster."

Sometimes Gracie would try skipping, but today she sat on her porch steps and complained about being left out.

From her perch in the tree, Ellen could see no more than a little bit of the sidewalk, so she only caught glimpses of the girls as they skipped or played hopscotch. Pearl and Jeanette were older than Gracie but younger than Charlene. Probably they were seven, she thought. They lived on the other side of the street, but they weren't sisters because when it was time to go home for lunch, they ran in different directions.

Unlike Gracie and Joey, Pearl and Jeanette did everything Charlene told them to do. They played the games she wanted to play and let her go first whenever she wanted to. They even went into the laneway behind the houses to tell Joey that his sister wanted him, even though they always said before they went, "But we're not allowed to go into the laneway."

"It'll only take you a minute," Charlene always answered. "Now go."

And they went.

Sitting up in the tree, Ellen thought, *I* wouldn't let her

boss *me* around like that. But she knew why they did what Charlene told them to. She remembered Peggy Scott who went to school with her at North Star country school. She was older than the other girls and she was good at all the games and always had interesting ideas for new games. Playing with Peggy was fun and exciting. Everyone wanted to play her games, so they let her boss them around.

Charlene was another girl who had interesting ideas. Today she decided that her front porch could be a stage and got all the girls to put on a play of "Goldilocks and the Three Bears."

"You can be Goldilocks," she said to Gracie. "It's the best part and you know the story, don't you?"

"Of course," said Gracie indignantly. "You've read it to me one hundred times."

"Good," said Charlene. "I'll be the biggest bear and you can be the middle bear, Jeanette. And you'll have to be the little bear, Pearl. Can you act little?"

"I can act *very* little," Pearl said in a high squeaky voice and giggled.

"We'll go through the play three times," said Charlene. "Then you two can go get the boys from the laneway to be the audience."

When the rehearsals were over, Pearl and Jeanette refused to go after the boys. "They won't come," they said.

"If you want them, you go get them."

Charlene sighed loudly and went. It was several minutes before she came back with five boys trailing behind her. Ellen saw them when they came around the house. She knew Joey when she saw his black hair sticking out from under his brown cap, but she had never seen the other boys before. They were all around Joey's age and did not seem too keen on seeing a play. Even Charlene couldn't get them to sit on the sidewalk to watch.

"We can see better if we stand up," Joey said flatly.

"Yes—and run away," said Charlene. "Promise to stay to the end and you'll each get a treat."

"Candy?" said the smallest boy eagerly.

"You'll see," said Charlene.

She ran up the steps. "Welcome to our play of 'Goldilocks and the Three Bears,'" she said in a deep voice and the play began.

From her branch, Ellen couldn't see the stage but she could hear the voices. She could also see the audience standing on the sidewalk, watching the play. At one point two of the boys started whispering, and Charlene came down from the stage to scold them.

"We're doing this for you," she said in a sharp voice, "and we expect you to listen. Do you understand?"

She sounds just like a teacher, thought Ellen.

The boys seemed to think so, too. "Yes ma'am," they said smartly and snickered. But after that they were quiet until the play was over. Then they said, "Now give us our treat. You promised us a treat."

Charlene reached into her pocket, took out a blue cardboard box, and shook it. It rattled. Ellen knew right away that it was gum, the kind with a white candy coating on the outside.

The boys held out their hands. Charlene rattled the box again. Then she carefully dropped one square white piece of gum into each waiting palm. The gum disappeared into mouths and the boys dashed off as fast as they could.

With the play over, the girls sat on the porch steps and one of them, Ellen couldn't tell whether it was Pearl or Jeanette, said, "What shall we do now?"

Charlene didn't answer for a long time. Then she said, "You decide. I'm fresh out of ideas."

Suddenly, Ellen felt like jumping down from the tree and saying, "I'll play with you! We could play hide-and-seek or 'Here I come, Where from?' Or you girls could draw with chalk on the sidewalk. Charlene and I want to talk."

But as soon as she thought it, she knew she couldn't. Of course she wouldn't jump down from the tree. That would be crazy and she would probably sprain her ankle or worse. It would make much more sense to walk downstairs and out the front door and talk to them, but she didn't have the courage to do that. What would she say? "Hi, I'm Ellen from Saskatchewan and I've been listening to you play for five days now."

She looked up into the branches of the tree. They made a world where she was safe and alone, listening in on the world of the street.

It is my listening tree, she thought. Up here, I can only listen. By listening I can get to know the kids down there, just a little, but they can't know me at all.

The thought made her feel lonely, and she scooted back along the branch and went downstairs to find herself some lunch.

CHAPTER 11

The next day at breakfast Aunt Gladys announced that the Third Floor Boys were coming back to Saskatchewan House that afternoon.

"There wasn't any work down on the docks the past couple of weeks so they've been helping their folks out in their gardens. They'll bring us some fresh vegetables and that's not all. They are going to bring six hens with them. So that will be a new chore for you, Ellen. I hope you're ready for it."

"Where are the chickens going to live?" asked Ellen, worried that Aunt Gladys didn't know that chickens would run away if they weren't fenced in.

"They'll live in the garage," said Aunt Gladys. "I don't use it since I have no car, and it's nice and airy. You can feed the hens our scraps and gather the eggs. You know how to get along with chickens. If they lay enough eggs, I can make a cake now and then."

Ellen remembered the chickens she had fed on the farm. There were a lot more than six and she was not very fond of their pushy ways. They scrabbled after food and sometimes pecked a person who was innocently gathering eggs. But she could do the job.

The Third Floor Boys turned out to be Tony and Al. Tony was tall and broad. Al was short and broad. They both had dark hair and eyes that crinkled up when they smiled.

"Are you sure you know enough to look after Lake Ontario chickens?" Al asked Ellen. "They learn a lot from the seagulls, you know. They're not just down-in-the-dirt farm chickens. They're always thinking about flying away."

"Let her alone," said Tony. "Chickens are chickens."

They took Ellen out to look at the garage. Right away she could see that any chickens who lived there would be pretty lucky. There was a rather dirty window that still let in plenty of light, and Tony had built boxes along one wall and put straw in them so the hens could lay eggs comfortably. There was a thick layer of straw on the dirt floor of the garage and a feeding trough and a pan for water.

"We found this old ladder and leaned it in the corner so these ladies will have a place to perch at night," said Al as he opened the box the hens had traveled in.

They came fluttering out. They were black and white, not the Rhode Island Reds Ellen was used to.

"They're Plymouth Rocks," said Tony, "but a chicken is a chicken, as I said before. You'll know how to take care of them, no problem."

"Aunt Gladys says I'm to feed them kitchen scraps. Will

that be enough?" asked Ellen. "On the farm, our chickens had lots of grasshoppers and grass seed to eat."

"We brought some chicken feed," said Al. "Give them a scoop of that and as many potato peelings and stale buns as you can and they'll be happy. And don't forget that they need water as well."

"It's funny to come to Toronto and feed chickens," Ellen said to Mama that evening. "Will Aunt Gladys be fussy about how I do it?"

Mama laughed. "My sister doesn't know anything about chickens," she said. "We grew up in Regina and I didn't know anything about farm animals either till I married a farmer. Just act as if you know what you're doing and you'll be fine. But don't forget to feed them. Chickens don't like to be hungry."

Ellen was surprised to find that living in a garage seemed to suit the chickens just fine. They didn't get very excited about the scoop of chicken feed, but when Ellen came with kitchen scraps they came toward her, clucking among themselves.

"It sounds as if they're talking to each other," Ellen told Mama, "wondering whether I've brought anything really good." She was getting to like these gossipy birds, and when she found two or three eggs in their nests she made sure to thank them.

One of the hens seemed to be the leader of the flock.

The "Queen Hen," Ellen called her. She was not the biggest but she was the fastest at getting to any especially delicious kitchen scraps. If another hen happened to get there first, the Queen Hen rushed up to her with wings outstretched and drove her away.

One morning, the Queen Hen looked over the scraps Ellen had scattered in the straw and seemed to decide that they weren't good enough for her. She lifted her head and saw that Ellen had left the garage door open. In a flash of feathers the hen was out through the opening. Ellen ran after her, slamming the door behind her.

The Queen Hen did not run into the garden to hide among the tomato plants. She dodged around the corner of the garage and ran down the narrow space between that garage and the one behind Charlene's house, dodging among the stems of the tall weeds. Ellen pushed her way through the weeds and found herself in a laneway lined with fences and garage doors.

The Queen Hen was walking now, turning her head from side to side, as if she was looking for something she recognized.

Maybe she's trying to get home to the country, thought Ellen. But how am I going to catch her? If I run after her, she'll run, too.

Just then a boy came out of the garage next door. It was

Joey, of course. The hen was right in front of him, and Joey stopped and stared. The Queen Hen stared back.

Joey looked around and saw Ellen.

"Is this yours?" he asked. "Did you bring it from Saskatchewan?"

"Of course not," said Ellen crossly. "I didn't bring anything but one suitcase. It's Aunt Gladys's hen. She escaped from the garage."

"She escaped? Then I'll catch her."

Ellen started to say, "Don't run." But she saw that Joey wasn't going to run after the Queen Hen. He was walking very slowly toward her. He was reaching into his pocket and pulling out a piece of toast. Just a crust really, but when the hen saw it she came toward Joey, dipping her head impatiently.

Joey held out the toast and glanced toward Ellen. "There," he said. "Now you have to pick her up. I'm not picking up any chicken."

Ellen went in a wide circle so that the Queen Hen wouldn't see her. When she was behind the hen she whispered, "Drop the toast on the ground."

As soon as the hen lowered her head toward the treat, Ellen scooped her up and held her close under her arm so that she couldn't push out with her wings.

"I'm putting her back in the garage right now," she said and made her way through the weeds and around the corner to the door, followed closely by Joey.

"Could you see that none of the others get out?" she asked him and opened the door a crack. The other hens were still busy pecking at the scraps on the floor and showed no interest in the return of their leader.

Joey, however, was interested.

"You got six of them," he said. "Are you going to eat them?"

"No," said Ellen. "They lay eggs and we eat the eggs."

"I know that eggs come from chickens," said Joey. "But we get our eggs from the store. Or at least, we did..." His voice trailed off.

Ellen looked at him. He was a skinny boy. He had probably given up the toast he had saved from breakfast so that she could catch the Queen Hen.

"Wait here," she said and went into the house. She took the lid off the biscuit tin that always stood on the kitchen counter. There were ginger cookies inside, she knew. Aunt Gladys doled them out one by one after dinner sometimes.

Aunt Gladys will understand when I tell her what happened, she thought and took two cookies out to Joey.

"Golly, thanks," he said.

"Well, thanks for helping. That was pretty smart of you to give her a treat. It can be really hard to catch a chicken," Ellen said. "If you run after them they just run faster."

"That's what I do, too, when someone's chasing me," said Joey. "I guess I understand chickens. Well, I got to go."

And he was gone, disappearing between the garages.

Ellen went back into the house. Maybe Joey wasn't so bad. But he wasn't about to become her friend.

CHAPTER 12

Ellen didn't see Joey again that day. Catching the Queen Hen made her late getting into the tree and by the time she got there Charlene and the other girls were sitting on the porch playing Tic-Tac-Toe where Ellen couldn't see them at all.

I wouldn't mind playing, though, thought Ellen. And we could try Hangman. But I guess Gracie couldn't play since she can't spell yet.

She stopped trying to catch glimpses of the girls and began to look high into the branches of the tree. A grey squirrel was running along a branch and when he came to the end of it, he leapt to another and then another until he was out of sight.

"I don't really belong in the listening tree," Ellen said to herself. "Not the way the squirrel does. All I can do is sit here." She closed her eyes and heard the tree rustling around her. "But it is beautiful."

She made her way back to her room and spent the rest of the day reading *Anne's House of Dreams*.

When Mama came home she said to Ellen, "I told Mrs. B. that I would come back this evening. She's having two old friends in for tea and cake after supper and she needs me to help. I probably won't be back till ten o'clock or so. Do you mind? You'll have to help the girls with tidying after dinner and then amuse yourself till I get home."

"I'll be fine," said Ellen. "I've started a new book."

Mama looked at the book and said, "It's a good one. If you fall asleep I'll turn out the light when I get home."

In the afternoon, Ellen went with Mama to a wonderful bakery to buy cakes for Mrs. B.'s party. Even though she had eaten a perfectly good lunch of chicken noodle soup and a cheese sandwich, the smell of baking made Ellen's mouth water. She tried not to look too longingly at the sugar cookies and cinnamon buns.

Mama bought little cakes frosted with pale yellow and pink and green icing, decorated with white curlicues. The bakery lady put them neatly into a box and folded white tissue paper around them.

Then she smiled at Ellen and said to Mama, "Would your little girl like a cookie?"

Ellen was not pleased to be called a little girl but she did want a cookie, so she smiled back and Mama said, "Thank you. I'm sure my daughter would love a cookie."

Ellen took the cookie and said, "Thank you very much."

The cookie was crisp on the edges and soft in the middle. She smiled at the woman again. When she was out on the street with Mama she said, "I guess when I'm not a little girl any more I won't get a cookie just for being polite."

"You're right," said Mama. "When you're older you'll have to work and buy your own treats."

"When will I be old enough to do that?"

"You're a bit young to get a job right now," said Mama. "But the way things are, a lot of children are working one way or another. Like your friend next door. She looks after her brother and sister while her mother works. She doesn't get paid but she's working just the same. And you do some work, too, feeding the chickens and helping Aunt Gladys."

She stopped right in the middle of the busy sidewalk and looked at Ellen. "I don't think you're a little girl at all. You're coping with a new place and new people and doing useful work. You're growing up."

Ellen was pleased, but inside she wondered whether a grown up girl would be spending so much time sitting in a tree. Then she thought of the green world of the listening tree. It was a good world to be in. But was it also a place to hide?

That evening Mama got straight up from the dinner table, picked up the bakery box and her handbag, and went off to help Mrs. B. with her tea party. The ABC girls cleared the table but Ellen said, "I'll help with the dishes tonight. I don't have anything important to do."

The young ladies bowed in unison and said, "Thank you,

Ellen," gave her three hugs, one after the other, and ran upstairs.

Ellen scraped the plates and stacked them carefully. Aunt Gladys put all the leftovers into bowls and set them in the icebox out on the back porch to keep cold until she decided what to do with them.

"Soup, I think," she said to Ellen. "Potatoes and green beans and carrots. A very good soup." She finished with a saying she repeated after every meal, "Waste not, want not. Remember that, Ellen."

"I'll remember," said Ellen and they tackled the dishes.

When they were finished, Mr. Martineau was still sitting at the dining table. He was playing solitaire, and when Ellen came in to get the salt and pepper shakers he surprised her by saying, "Would you like to play a game of rummy?"

Ellen had played rummy with Dad and Mama but she found that Mr Martineau was a much trickier player. He would hold sets of cards in his hand, then suddenly put them all down at once and "go out," leaving Ellen with many cards that counted against her. At first Ellen was annoyed, but then she began to hold cards herself and several times her opponent was caught with a hand full of kings and queens.

Mr. Martineau said, "Good work, young lady. If you want to win you have to take some chances. But you also have to know when to make your move. Don't wait too long or you'll lose everything. I learned that the hard way, but maybe you can learn it playing rummy." He squared the deck of cards neatly. "I look forward to our next game."

Ellen went up to her own room. It wasn't nearly bedtime and she was restless. She didn't feel like reading so she stepped over to the window and looked out into the listening tree.

It was dusk, now. A streetlight had come on but its yellow glow barely penetrated the thick foliage of the tree. She could make out the shape of the grey branches but the leaves were just a dark mass. What would it be like to sit in the tree as it grew dark?

I'd be like a bird in its nest, getting ready to go to sleep, thought Ellen. I'd better try it now. I might never get another chance.

Quickly, she opened the window and carefully crossed the roof. When she touched the thick branch, it was still warm from the sun. It was just as easy to climb onto it in the darkness and move along it, away from the house, as it was in daylight. When she got to the place where the branch forked, she stopped, reached out for the small branch, and held on firmly so she wouldn't fall into the darkness.

She listened. The street was very quiet. She could hear footsteps somewhere nearby and music playing far away, but the daytime sounds of children shouting and adults talking were gone.

There was a small breeze and the leaves of the tree

rustled all around her, but gently. The sound was comforting, as if she was enclosed by something warm and friendly. Ellen could feel her eyes closing. There was nothing to see, anyway, out here in the darkness.

But I mustn't fall asleep, she thought, and tightened her hand around the branch. If I fall, I'll have to explain where I fell from. That would be too embarrassing.

She thought of the squirrels who must be asleep in their nests high in the tree. "They belong here. I'm just a visitor," she said under her breath.

Ellen was almost ready to start moving back toward the roof when she was startled to hear a voice below her.

It was a man's voice, a voice that definitely did not want to be overheard. It was almost a whisper, but in the quiet of evening Ellen could hear it. It said, "You don't mean this big house, do you?"

Another voice answered. This voice was quiet, too, but so deep it seemed to rumble through the wood of the tree. It said, "No, it's the two-story job next door. She lives there with her three kids."

Three kids. That meant Charlene, Joey, and Gracie. Ellen felt as if she was listening with her whole body. She had to understand what the whisper and the rumble were saying.

The whisper asked, "How much money does she owe?"

The rumble answered, "Forty dollars. She has a job now

and she gave me five dollars the other day, but I'm not in the charity business."

"She knows she owes it?"

"Sure she does. I told her it all has to be paid now. She says she doesn't have it. She'll pay it off five dollars at a time. Has to feed her kids. You know the story."

"I've heard it before." There was a pause and then the whisper went on. "Does the old lady know you want to evict this family?"

"She doesn't want to know a thing about the people renting the house," the rumble answered. "She just wants the rent. I'll tell her that the tenants won't pay. She won't like that. If I tell her I've got an eviction order, she'll go for it."

"I'll notify the police. They are the ones to serve the eviction order. They can do it later this week. Then the tenant has one month to come up with the cash. All forty dollars of it."

"She won't be able to do it." The deep voice was so pleased that Ellen wished she had something heavy to drop on the man's head or at least his toes. But he was still talking. "After the woman and her kids get out I'll work on the old lady to sell the place. I'll give her some story about how I can't get tenants who will pay the rent. She doesn't know what's going on and I'll make sure she sells it to you cheap. You have my word."

The whisper sounded pleased, too. "If I get the house for

a low price there'll be something in it for you."

"It'll be easy. What does she know, stuck away in that big house?"

"Just get the job done. I'll let you know about the eviction. It may take a few days."

There was a pause, and then the deep voice answered, "I'd like to get this family out fast. I might just put a little scare into them. Once the house is empty I can start telling the old lady it's a good idea for her to sell it."

"Humph," said the whispery voice. "Just don't do anything stupid."

Then Ellen heard footsteps walking away. One set going south and the other going north.

As soon as she couldn't hear them any more she loosened her grip on the small branch. She had been holding on so tight that her fingers were numb. She wiggled them until they worked again, then she scooted herself back to the roof and climbed in through the window.

She turned out the light and undressed quickly. Usually she left the window open a crack so that she could feel the cool night breeze and hear it shake the leaves of the tree. Tonight she shut the window tight. She didn't want to risk hearing those voices again.

But the voices stayed in her head. Especially one word. Eviction.

When Mama came in from Mrs. B.'s she poked her head through the curtain and whispered, "Are you asleep, Ellen?"

"Not really," said Ellen, feeling very glad to hear a familiar and kind voice.

Her mother came in and sat on her bed. "Are you thinking about something?"

"Eviction." The word popped out of Ellen's mouth.

"Eviction!" said Mama. "What made you think about that?"

"I just heard someone talking about it today," said Ellen.

"I'm not surprised," said Mama. "A lot of people are having trouble paying their rent. And the landlords want them out if they can't pay. That's eviction. They hardly give people a chance, even in these hard times. And where are they to go?"

She reached out and patted Ellen on the shoulder. "But you don't have to worry about eviction, honey. Gladys would never evict us, and I can save enough to pay the taxes on the farm at the end of the year, so it's safe. Now, go to sleep."

She got up and went back through the curtain to her room. Ellen did go to sleep, but her last thought was almost worse than the thought of eviction. Tomorrow she would have to go out on the street and talk to Charlene. Charlene had to know what Ellen had heard.

CHAPTER 13

In the morning, as she dried the dishes, Ellen almost told Aunt Gladys about the eviction. She was a grownup. She might know what to do. But in her heart Ellen knew that she had to tell Charlene before she did anything else. She set the oatmeal pot down with a thump. Her mind was made up.

"Are you worried about something?" asked Aunt Gladys suddenly, startling her. "You keep muttering under your breath."

"Just something I was trying to figure out," said Ellen. But Aunt Gladys was already putting the last of the dishes away and preparing to go down to her hidey-hole in the basement. She wasn't really interested.

Neither were the chickens, but they didn't mind listening as Ellen fed them and explained that she had to tell Charlene that her family might be evicted.

One of the hens cocked its head and made a clucking sound, so Ellen went on, "I'll tell her the truth about what the men said but maybe I don't need to tell her about the listening tree."

The chickens seemed to approve, but Ellen felt very uncomfortable as she went out the front door and stood on the porch. She looked at the little house next door. There was no one to be seen. She sat on the top step of Saskatchewan House to wait.

Maybe they've gone somewhere for the day, she thought hopefully and immediately told herself not to be such a coward. Then she heard a voice.

"It's about time you came out of that house," it said. Ellen jumped. She knew it was Charlene's voice. She had heard it so many times before. She looked around and saw Charlene standing on the curb across the street, staring at her. Her eyes were dark brown and bright, and her hair was almost red in the morning sun.

"Your aunt told us you were coming and I thought, finally, there would be a girl who didn't need looking after. Someone who could just play. But then you never came out. What good is that?"

Ellen couldn't think what to say but Charlene had only paused for breath anyway.

"How old are you?" she asked bluntly.

That was a question Ellen could answer. "Nine going on ten," she said.

"Not too bad," said Charlene. "I just turned ten, myself." She chewed her bottom lip for a moment and then seemed to make up her mind. "I know your name is Ellen. Well, mine is Charlene."

Ellen almost said, "I already knew that," but she stopped herself in time and remembered why she was there on the porch instead of up in the tree.

"I'm glad you're by yourself, Charlene," she said. "I have something to tell you."

Charlene looked surprised. "Just me?" she asked.

"Yes," said Ellen. "Just you."

"I'm coming over," said Charlene. She crossed the street and stood in front of Ellen. "You'd better talk fast because I have to go get Gracie in a minute. She's my sister and she went to see a kitten Jeanette found."

"All right," Ellen said. "I have to tell you that I heard two men talking last night. They were standing under this tree and I could hear them. They said that your family is going to be evicted. I had to tell you so I came out to find you."

Charlene stood still as a statue for a minute. Then she asked, "How do you know they were talking about us?"

"They said it was the little house, not this big one, and that the woman has three kids."

Charlene sat down on the bottom step. Ellen was behind her and couldn't see her face, but Charlene was sitting stiffly, as if she was about to ward off a blow.

"That's us, all right," she said. "My mum has been worrying about it. She doesn't say but I see her counting her pay and figuring how to make it stretch. She was out of work for two months and now she can't catch up."

"Where will you go?" asked Ellen. "I mean, if you do get evicted."

"We'll probably flit before they evict us. That way we can take our furniture to sell to get some money for a deposit on a new place. It's our furniture, but if they come to evict us they'll throw it out on the street and bust it up." She thumped her fist on the step beside her. "Then we'll have to find some cheaper place. Maybe one room. It's not right! I'll have to watch Gracie and Joey in some stinking room. Why can't they leave us alone?"

She stopped talking and hunched her shoulders. Ellen waited. She had no idea what to say now.

At last, Charlene got up and began stamping up and down the front walk, away from Ellen and then toward her. She finally stopped at the bottom of the steps and said, "So, where's your dad?"

Ellen was startled. She had not expected this question but she was glad that she could answer it. "He's up north in Alberta, doing farm work. Our farm in Saskatchewan dried up and he went off in a boxcar looking for work. We didn't know where he was until just the other day. It was awful."

"Do you think he'll come back?"

Ellen stared at Charlene. She had never thought that her dad might not come back. She worried that something terrible might happen to him, but she knew he would come back if he could.

"He'll come back," she said firmly. "He will. When times get better. He already sent us some money and I know he'll come back."

"Well, my dad won't," said Charlene. "He left in the middle of the night. The cops were after him for some stupid thing he did. He'll never come back and now we're going to get evicted." She sat down again and hid her face in her hands.

Ellen looked down at her for a minute. Then she came down the steps and sat beside her.

It's true, Ellen thought unhappily. Nothing is right. Dad had to go away and then Mama and me had to leave too, and go far away in a different direction. Charlene's father is gone and now these men are plotting to take away their home. Plotting right under the listening tree. What right do they have to evict a whole family?

"Charlene," she said. "Listen. We can't do anything about our dads. My mother and I only came here because we had to, but what's happening to you is worse. You shouldn't be evicted. We can't let it happen."

Charlene shrugged and Ellen went on, "You weren't even surprised when I told you that someone was planning to have you evicted. You know who those men are, don't you? Tell me. Who are they?"

Charlene took her hands away from her face and looked at Ellen. "I don't know about *two* men," she said. "But I'm sure of one. It's Mr. Bragg. He's the one who collects the rent. He always yells at Mum about the rent she can't pay and says she better watch out or he'll kick us out and sell the house. He never listens to anything she says. Just slams the door and stomps away. He's a bully."

"Does he have a very deep raspy voice?"

Charlene nodded. "He sounds like an old bullfrog."

"He's the one who wants to get you evicted. The other man had a whispery voice. He wants you out so he can get his hands on your house."

"What does that mean?" asked Charlene.

"He wants to buy it for a cheap price."

"But the old lady will never sell," said Charlene. "That's what Mum always tells us when Mr. Bragg has been trying to scare us. The old lady is the one who owns the house. Mr. Bragg just collects money for her."

"The old lady!" said Ellen. "Those two men talked about the old lady. They said she forgets things and doesn't want to be bothered. Mr. Bragg is going to talk her into selling. But who is she?"

"How would I know?" said Charlene. "She never comes here. Just gets our money."

"Maybe she lives far away," said Ellen.

"No, she lives up by the castle. Do you know where that is?"

"I do," said Ellen. "My mother works up there in some big house. For an old lady…" For a moment she could feel her brain clicking away. Then she said, "Charlene, stay here. I have to go talk to Aunt Gladys. Don't go away."

"I have to get Gracie," said Charlene. "But after that I don't have anywhere to go. I'll be here. Just promise that you'll come back and tell me what's going on."

"I will," said Ellen. "I promise."

CHAPTER 14

Ellen stood in the front hall of Saskatchewan House and tried to get her thoughts to make sense. Aunt Gladys had said that Mama might get a job with an old neighbour of hers. Could Mrs. B. and the owner of Charlene's house be the same person?

There was nothing to do but ask Aunt Gladys. Ellen didn't stop to think that her aunt wanted to be left alone after her morning's work was done. She forgot that even Mama had never been in her sister's rooms in the basement. She had to talk to Aunt Gladys *right now*.

She ran through the house and out onto the back porch. There beside the big wooden icebox was a door. She opened it and saw a narrow flight of stairs leading down to another door. In the dim light she could see a large brass knocker, shining against the dark wood of the door. She hurried down the stairs. Even in her excitement she noticed that the knocker was fashioned in the shape of a lion's head. This was not an ordinary basement door. That was for sure.

She knocked twice, very gently, but the sharp sound seemed loud in the small space at the foot of the stairs. After a moment, the door opened a crack.

"What on earth?" said Aunt Gladys. "I thought I made it perfectly clear that I am never to be bothered when I'm in my own quarters."

She started to close the door but Ellen said quickly, "I'm sorry, Aunt Gladys. I have a very, very important question and no one else can answer it. It's about the house next door."

"Where the Kennedys live? All right," said her aunt. "You look upset. You had better come in—but don't expect to be invited back. I never allow anyone to invade my privacy."

She pulled Ellen through the door and shut it behind her. Ellen blinked. It was quite dark, but a lamp with a golden glass shade shed a glowing light on a red velvet sofa and a rug with an intricate red-and-gold pattern. Aunt Gladys's hidey-hole was full of shiny and soft things.

Ellen shook her head. She couldn't get distracted now. She had to ask the question.

Aunt Gladys thought so, too. "You'd better spit it out, girl," she said. "What do you want to ask me?"

Ellen took a deep breath. "Do you know the family next door?"

"Of course. That poor Mrs. Kennedy. She's having a hard time now that her husband has gone off."

"That's what Charlene said." Ellen didn't want Aunt Gladys to waste time explaining the Kennedys to her so she rushed on. "Now they've heard that they might be evicted because the woman who owns the house wants to sell it. Do you think it could be true? Do you know her?"

Aunt Gladys sat down on the red velvet sofa. "Of course I know her," she said. "Or I used to when she lived next door. That was before my husband died. She was a widow with a daughter and we were quite friendly. But she's lived up by Casa Loma for years, now. We kind of lost touch."

"It's Mrs. B. isn't it?" Ellen asked eagerly. "Mrs. Bartholomew—the woman Mama works for. Is she the old lady who owns the house?"

"Well, she wouldn't appreciate being called 'the old lady,'" said Aunt Gladys. "But yes, she owns the house. I didn't tell Martha about it because Mrs. B. doesn't like people to know that she was once a poor widow living in a small ordinary house, but that's what she was. She lived there for years. Now she doesn't want to set eyes on it—but I can promise you that she won't sell it."

"But why? She can't care about it much."

"She cares about it but she's ashamed of it, too," said Aunt Gladys. "She caught the eye of wealthy Mr. Bartholomew who married her and took her to live up by Casa Loma. Her big house and her money came from Mr. B. But that little house was hers and she kept it. She still owns it, and now she can sit back like a lady and collect the rent. That's what she wants to do. Why would she sell it for practically nothing? That's all she would get these days. And I expect that the money Mr. B. left isn't worth so much any more. So she may even need the rent."

She looked at Ellen and frowned. "Who's saying that she wants to sell?"

Ellen had to think fast. "Well, Charlene heard that the man who collects the rent is talking about it."

Aunt Gladys slapped her hand on the velvet cushion beside her. "It's that Bragg fellow," she said. "He's a slippery one. He did some business for Mrs. B.'s husband and she hasn't seen fit to get rid of him. He's probably feeding her some lies about this being a good time to sell. And he'll try to cheat her out of money into the bargain. No doubt of that."

Ellen gave a quiet sigh of relief. She didn't have to explain how Charlene heard about Mr. Bragg's plan. But now Aunt Gladys was fixing her with a beady eye.

"Someone has to tell Mrs. B. what's happening," she said. She closed her eyes and Ellen could see that she was thinking very hard. She shook her head twice and then opened her eyes. "Ellen, I'm afraid you're the one to do it."

Ellen stopped feeling relieved. "Me! Why am I the one to do it? I don't even know Mrs. B."

"That's why you're perfect," Aunt Gladys said in a firm voice. "You're a polite girl. You wrote her a nice thank-you note for the dresses. She likes your mother and she doesn't know you personally, so she has nothing against you."

She seemed to realize that she needed to explain and went on, "You see, Mrs. B. finds fault with people. She stopped being friendly with me when I decided to turn my house into a boarding house. She thinks boarding houses are very low class. So I can't talk to her about this problem. She likes your mother but if your mother gets mixed up in anything about the house, she would be accused of meddling and likely get fired. But Mrs. B. can't fire you, and she does care about her little house. If you tell her what's going on, I believe she'll listen and she'll do something about it."

"Maybe Mrs. Kennedy should talk to her," said Ellen desperately. "She's the one who would get evicted."

"Mrs. Kennedy would just remind Mrs. B. of the time she was poor and living in that house all alone with her little girl. She wouldn't talk to her at all. No, you're the one."

Ellen felt a little dizzy. Surely some grownup should talk to Mrs. B. But who could it be? Not Aunt Gladys and not Mama and not Charlene's mother.

She remembered the voices of the men under the tree. The rough one and the whispery one.

I heard those men, she told herself. They don't care about anything except getting that house. I can't let them get away with it. I have to talk to Mrs. B.

"All right," she said to her aunt. "I'll do it."

Aunt Gladys said, "You had better plan to go tomorrow. I know that Martha is going shopping for Mrs. B. tomorrow morning, so you'll be able to talk to her alone."

"Will she open the door? It sounds as if she's not very friendly."

"She's not friendly but she's lonely. She'll want to know why you're there. So get her interested right away. If you're clever she'll listen to you."

Aunt Gladys stood up. "It's up to you. Now run along. And remember this room is my sanctuary. I don't want you talking about it. You are only here because of extraordinary circumstances. Do you understand?"

"Yes, Aunt Gladys. But it's beautiful. That lamp with the golden glass shade and all the pillows. It's elegant."

Aunt Gladys looked pleased. "It's a little piece of my old life," she said. "Before my husband died and before this terrible Depression, this whole house was elegant. That lamp with the golden shade was a wedding present from my husband. I remember how much your mother loved it when he gave it to me. She was just twelve then. Someday I'll show her that I still have it."

She looked around at the red velvet sofa and all the shiny vases and candlesticks. "I do need this little bit of elegance every day," she said.

"Mama calls it your hidey-hole," said Ellen. "Well, I think it's beautiful."

"My what?" her aunt exclaimed. Her voice was horrified, but then she laughed. "My hidey-hole! Only Martha would think of that. Just remember, Ellen. It's my secret."

Ellen took one more look at red velvet and golden light before the door closed behind her and all she could see of gold was a door-knocker shaped like a lion's head.

As she walked up the narrow stairs the green world of the listening tree came into her mind. The tree is *my* hidey-hole, she thought. It's my special place and no one else ever goes there. They don't even know about it. I have a secret, too.

CHAPTER 15

Ellen came out on the porch of Saskatchewan House and looked over at Charlene who was sitting on the bottom step next door. Gracie was sitting beside her and Joey was just coming up the street calling out, "Lunch time! What's for lunch, Charlene?"

Could it really be lunch time? Ellen jumped down the last three steps and went over to stand in front of Charlene. "Sit down, Joey," she said. "I have something to tell all of you. It's more important than lunch."

Joey stared at her for a minute and then sat down with a thump.

"Where did you come from all of a sudden?" he asked.

"Never mind about that now," said Ellen. "Listen. I already told Charlene that I found out you are going to be evicted."

Joey looked at Charlene who nodded glumly. "It's that Mr. Bragg," she said. "Mama's behind on the rent."

Joey jumped up. "He can't do that," he said in a fierce voice. "It's not even his house."

"I know," said Ellen. "He doesn't own the house, but he

thinks he can get you out and then convince the owner to sell it. He's got a friend waiting to buy the house cheap and Mr. Bragg will make some money out of the deal. The owner doesn't know anything about their wicked plan."

She stopped for a moment. She must have read the words "wicked plan" in some story. But this was wicked. It really was. She went on. "So I have to tell the owner what Mr. Bragg is doing. If I tell her, maybe she won't sell the house and you won't be evicted."

Charlene said in a flat voice, "This doesn't make any sense. We don't even know who the owner is. Just that it's an old woman."

"I *do* know who she is," said Ellen. "Aunt Gladys told me. She's Mrs. Bartholomew, the woman my mother works for. She lives right up by Casa Loma. Aunt Gladys will give me the address. She says that I'm the one to tell Mrs. Bartholomew what's going on, and I have to do it tomorrow."

Charlene and Joey both stared at her. Joey said, "Tomorrow? You have to do it tomorrow?"

"Yes, I do. Because there's no time to waste. These men want you out fast. And tomorrow morning Mama will be out shopping so I can talk to Mrs. B. alone. Aunt Gladys is afraid that Mama might get fired if Mrs. B. thinks she's meddling in her affairs."

Charlene looked at Joey. "We're the ones being evicted.

We should go talk to her. Not Ellen."

"Yeah," said Joey. "We have to." But Ellen knew that he didn't like the idea very much.

"Look," she said. "I have to go. Aunt Gladys used to be her friend. And she likes Mama. That might make her want to talk to me. But it would be much, *much* better if you were there, too." She felt a rush of relief. She would not have to do it alone.

"Me, too," said Gracie. "I want to see the big house."

"We'll all go," said Charlene. She looked critically at her brother and sister. "We have to look respectable. Gracie, you can wear your pink dress that used to be mine and you'll look like any mother's dream. But what will I wear?"

Ellen remembered the dresses from Mrs. B. The ones that were just a little too big for her. "I have a dress you can wear. It has red and brown stripes. I'll bring it over."

"Thanks," said Charlene. "That's me taken care of. But what about you?" She poked Joey in the stomach. "Just find something clean."

She suddenly turned so she could look straight at Gracie. "We can't tell Mum. It's okay for us to go because Ellen's aunt knows, but you mustn't tell Mum. We'll tell her about it later when we find out what Mrs. B. is going to do. Do you promise?"

Gracie nodded solemnly.

"Good. But I won't let you out of my sight once Mum gets home tonight. You might forget." She turned to Ellen. "We'll be back before lunch, right? We won't be gone long?"

"I'm sure we won't," said Ellen. "We don't have that much to say." It suddenly seemed to her that they had practically nothing to say that Mrs. B. would care about at all. Then she remembered what Mr. Martineau said to her when they were playing rummy.

"If we're going to stop these men we have to take a chance," she said. "And we can't wait. We have to tell her now or you'll be evicted almost for sure. We have to do it."

They all nodded.

Then Joey said, "Hey, I'm hungry. What about lunch?"

In the morning, as soon as Mama had gone off to the shops for Mrs. B., Ellen put on the blue dress with tulip buttons. When she met the others on the front walk, Gracie looked like a picture in a pink organdy dress with a ruffled skirt. Charlene was wearing the striped brown and red dress, and Joey was amazingly neat in blue short trousers and a light blue shirt.

"I remembered our first-day-of-school clothes," Charlene said. "Mama got them at a church sale and put them away so we wouldn't ruin them. We'll put Joey's outfit right back when we come home." She looked sternly at Joey. "Mind you don't fall down. I want no rips."

They all walked slowly over to Bathurst Street and then up the hill.

"We ought to have a plan," said Ellen.

"You talk first," said Charlene. "Because of Aunt Gladys and your mother. You can introduce yourself."

"Then I just have to tell her what I heard," said Ellen. "That's what she needs to know and then you can talk, too. So she'll know that you are the people who live in the house, the one she owns."

"I hope this is going to work," said Charlene, but very quietly so that only Ellen heard her.

They kept walking more and more slowly, but no matter how they dragged their feet they came much too soon to a big house with number 43 on it—the address Aunt Gladys had given Ellen.

Joey looked around the wide front lawn circled by tall trees and dark green shrubs and said, "Our whole house could fit in this front yard and it wouldn't squash anything. There's nothing but grass. No flowers."

"There are no flowers because Mrs. B. doesn't like colour," said Ellen. "I hope she doesn't mind our clothes. And I have to remember to say 'Mrs. Bartholomew' when I talk to her. I don't think she would like being called Mrs. B."

The house in front of them was built of grey stone. It had wide windows on either side of a tall front door painted black. Above the porch roof was a row of windows with small panes of glass, and another row above that with little gables even higher.

The children went up the grand steps and stood close together on the stone verandah in front of that tall black door. Then Joey stepped forward and lifted the big iron knocker. It landed with such a loud thump that all the children jumped.

The door opened instantly and Mrs. Bartholomew stood looking down at them. She was tall and thin, wearing a gray dress and a paler gray shawl. Her hair was white and she wore round, silver-rimmed glasses. She stood very straight and looked at the children and frowned.

"I think I know who you are," she said to Ellen. "Your mother told me that you like that blue dress. It was a favourite of my grandaughter's, too. But you other three are strangers to me. Are you collecting for something? I never give at the door." She started to close the heavy door.

Ellen took a step forward. "We aren't collecting for anything, Mrs. Bartholomew," she said. "You're right. I'm Ellen Jackson. We came to tell you something important."

"Does your mother know you are here?"

"No, but my Aunt Gladys does. She suggested we come and talk to you."

"Your aunt is not a fool," said Mrs. B. "We have practically nothing in common, but she has good sense. She wouldn't send you to bother me if it wasn't important. You had better come in."

She led them through a front hall paved with black-and-white marble into a small room crowded with plants. There were large pots holding tree-sized plants and smaller pots sitting on white wicker tables. There were also plants in baskets hanging from the high ceiling. All of the plants were green. There were no flowers. The air felt heavy and damp.

Mrs. Bartholomew sat down on the only chair in the room.

The children lined up in front of her. Ellen looked down at Gracie who was standing between her and Charlene. She was shaking a little and Charlene reached over and took her hand.

"You came to tell me something," said Mrs. Bartholomew. "Tell me."

Ellen tried to remember that Mrs. B. was lonely and bored. She would listen as long as Ellen had something interesting to say. She thought of the voices of the two men: the rumble and the whisper. For a moment she remembered holding her breath and the feel of the rough bark of the tree and the leaves around her.

She said, "Two nights ago I heard two men talking in front of Aunt Gladys's house. It was dark and I couldn't see them, but one had a loud rough voice and the other had a whispery voice. The one with the rough voice wants to evict the family that lives in the little house next to Aunt Gladys's."

"I own that house," said Mrs. B., sitting up even straighter.

"And we live in it," said Charlene. "Me and Gracie and Joey and our mum."

"Oh, I see," said Mrs. B. "That's who you are."

Ellen went on, "One man told the other that the woman who lives there is behind in her rent because she was out of a job for a while. She's trying to pay but she has to feed her kids."

"Humph," said Mrs. B. "And I need my rent."

"But that's not all," said Ellen quickly. "He told the other man that he can talk the old lady who owns the house into selling it cheap. He said he can talk her into anything."

Mrs. B. leaned forward. "He said what?" she asked sharply.

Ellen took a deep breath. "He said he could talk you into anything."

"He's wrong about that," said Mrs. B. "Talk me into anything. Ridiculous. He just brings me the rent money. But why would he want to buy that little house?"

"He doesn't," said Ellen. "It's the other man. He wants it if he can get it really cheap."

Charlene said, "And the man who collects the rent said it would be no problem because you stay in this big house and you don't know what's going on."

Mrs. B. didn't say anything. She sat absolutely still. Ellen held her breath and she could tell that Charlene wasn't breathing either. Then all of a sudden, Mrs. B. laughed. It was such a delighted laugh that Ellen found herself smiling, too, though she had no idea why.

Mrs. B. stopped laughing. "Bragg thinks that because I choose to stay in my house and I lose my glasses from time to time that I'm an old fool. But when I find my glasses I read the newspaper, and I know how much my house is worth. I'm not going to sell it. It doesn't matter what he says. That is my house and I will keep it."

Ellen waited, hoping Mrs. B. would say something about the eviction. After a short silence she knew that she would have to ask.

But it was Charlene who spoke up. "Can Mr. Bragg evict us without even asking you? Like you said, it's not his house—it's yours."

Mrs. B. frowned. "Do you know how much back rent your mother owes?"

"He said Mrs. Kennedy owes forty dollars in back rent," said Ellen. "She pays him five dollars whenever she can."

"She's working now," said Joey.

Mrs. B. shook her head. "I don't want to evict you," she said. "But your mother owes the rent. The question is—will she pay it all in the end?"

"Of course we will," said Charlene fiercely. Ellen frowned

at her. They didn't want to make Mrs. B. angry.

Joey was jiggling up and down. "We'll make the money. Me and Charlene. We can earn enough. We can figure out how to do it." He looked over at Charlene. "We can, can't we?"

"Sure," said Charlene.

"I'll help, too," said Ellen. But she wondered, *how*? How can we make that much money when men can't get jobs?

Mrs. B. was nodding. "All right," she said. "If the back rent is paid by the end of the year you will not be evicted."

Ellen was so surprised that she hardly noticed when Mrs. B. stood up and shooed them all into the front hall.

"Go along," she said. "I can promise you Kennedy children one thing: Mr. Bragg won't bother your mother any more. But she still owes me forty dollars."

She opened the door and the children stepped out onto the stone veranda.

"Wait," said Mrs. B. "I don't say thank you very often, but I do thank the four of you for telling me about that Mr. Bragg. Thinking I'm an old fool! He has a big surprise coming."

She started to shut the door, but Gracie looked up at her and said, "You're welcome," just before the door closed with a thump.

"Good for you, Gracie," said Charlene. "At least one of us has not forgotten how to be polite." She looked at Ellen and

Joey. "She *did* say that we will not be evicted right now. She *did* say that, didn't she?"

"Yes!" said Ellen and Joey and Gracie, all together.

They looked at each other and grinned. But they didn't shout "Hooray!" There was that little matter of forty dollars to think about.

CHAPTER 16

The children went down the steps and down the front walk. When they got to the street they turned toward home without talking. They had made a promise. How could they keep it?

Suddenly Ellen said, "Could we go by Casa Loma? I've never seen it close up."

"Sure," said Joey. "We just turn left here instead of going over to Bathurst. I can tell you a lot about the castle."

He sounded proud, as if he was about to show off something of his own.

They crossed one street and then another and there it was: a very big stone house with towers rising from its roof and a wall around the whole thing. The towers and the wall turned it into a castle.

Joey led them up to a heavy wooden gate across the drive that went up to the front door. Some of the boards had fallen out, and Ellen could see a dry fountain and cracked pavement. Weeds had pushed their way through the cracks.

Still, it was a castle. It felt surprising to be living in the neighbourhood of any castle, even one that was abandoned.

"It's a bit like Sleeping Beauty's castle after all the people in it have been asleep for a hundred years," said Ellen. "Do you really go into the garden, Joey?"

"Sometimes," said Joey. "But not through this gate. There's a watchman around sometimes. I climb over the wall."

They began to walk down the curved street that followed the castle wall. The wall was much taller than Ellen but she could see that the hollows left by fallen stones would make perfect foot and hand holds for any good climber.

I could probably do it, she thought, remembering the barn. I'm a good climber.

Joey lifted his foot and put it into one of the hollows and reached for another crevice with his hand. "See?" he said. "This is how I get over the wall."

"But you're not supposed to," said Charlene.

Joey jumped away from the wall and ran down the hill ahead of the girls. He came to a wooden door in the wall where he stopped and waited for them.

"Look," he said. "It's not quite closed. We could go in." He put his hand on the door.

"I want to," said Gracie. "I want to see the castle."

"We've seen it," said Charlene.

"It's better from the garden," said Joey.

"I want to go in, too," said Ellen. "I don't think there's anyone around."

"I hope not," said Charlene. "If we get caught, I'm the one in big trouble." But she was the one who pushed the door open.

They stepped into a thick wall of bushes.

"We just have to push our way through," said Joey.

"No," said Charlene. "We can't tear our good clothes. Look—there's sort of a path along the wall."

By going in single file and pushing branches aside with their hands, the children made their way along the wall in the direction of the castle. Suddenly the bushes stopped.

"There's grass here, just below the terrace," said Joey.

The grass was knee high and full of weeds, but Ellen barely noticed. She was looking up at a stone terrace with big windows behind it. Behind the windows were blinds, but she could imagine how beautiful it would be if the blinds were open and the rooms were filled with lamps shining out onto the terrace. It really was like Sleeping Beauty's castle, only with thick bushes instead of briars.

"They must have had parties on the terrace," she said.

"They did," said Joey. "We found a lot of wine bottles in that big heap over there." He pointed toward a big pile of rubble at the end of the terrace.

"Just junk," said Charlene.

"There's good stuff in there," said Joey. "Boards and wooden boxes and even some pots and pans and dishes. Somebody must have cleared out the kitchen and dumped everything."

"Is this where you got that candle holder you gave Mum for her birthday?" Charlene gave Joey a stern look.

"Yeah," said Joey. "Like I said, there's lots of interesting stuff." He looked defiantly at Charlene. "They already had a big sale and sold anything they could. Nobody cares about what's left."

Ellen was still looking at the curtained windows. Suddenly, she saw one of the curtains move. The light glinted as the window slowly opened. For a tiny moment she thought that a lady in a ball gown would step out onto the terrace. Then she realized that it must be the watchman.

"Someone's coming out on the terrace," she whispered.

Joey took a quick look. "Just stay right under the terrace wall till we get to the bushes," he said in a low voice. "He won't come down into the garden. They never do."

The children ran as quietly as they could, but to Ellen the crack of dry sticks under their feet sounded as loud as thunder. They got to the door in the wall and stepped through, out onto the sidewalk.

Joey pulled the door shut. "They should be careful about locking this," he said. "Anyone could get in."

Ellen looked at him. He was perfectly serious. It's like the castle is *his*, she thought. He doesn't want just anyone getting into the garden.

Charlene was busy brushing twigs and leaves off of her dress and Joey's shirt. "No rips," she said. "Thank goodness. And your dress looks fine, too, Gracie. I don't want Mum wondering how we managed to mess up our clothes when we aren't even supposed to be wearing them."

Ellen brushed off her own dress. The hem was coming down but she wasn't worried. She could fix that herself.

The four of them walked the rest of the way home in silence.

When Ellen got back to Saskatchewan House she was surprised to find Mama sitting at the table having a cup of tea with Aunt Gladys.

"Mrs. B.'s shopping didn't take me long, so I stopped off to have a short visit before I go up the hill. Where have you been? I found Gladys doing the dishes by herself."

Ellen looked at Aunt Gladys who nodded and said, "I'll tell you why I sent Ellen off this morning. Then Ellen can tell us what she's been doing. That will be very interesting, I promise you."

She poured a cup of tea, put in a lot of milk, and passed it across the table to Ellen who drank it down thankfully. She was glad that her aunt was going to do some of the explaining.

She listened while Aunt Gladys told Mama about the plot by Mr. Bragg and another man to get the Kennedys evicted. She finished by saying, "You see, Martha, that house belongs to Mrs. B. I knew that I couldn't get mixed up in this and neither could you, so I told Ellen that she was the one to talk to Mrs. B."

Mama raised her eyebrows and looked at Ellen, but Aunt Gladys went on. "Now we can hear what Mrs. B. had to say. Tell us, Ellen."

"I didn't go alone," said Ellen. "Charlene and Joey and Gracie went, too. They said that they were the ones that would be evicted so they wanted to have their say."

"What about Mrs. B?" asked Aunt Gladys impatiently. "Did she listen to you?"

"She listened," said Ellen. "And she promised not to evict the Kennedys as long as they pay her the forty dollars in back rent."

"That's good, Ellen. You must have done a good job of talking. But what about Bragg? What did she say about him?"

"She laughed, Aunt Gladys. She really laughed when we told her that Mr. Bragg thought she didn't know anything and he could get her to do whatever he wanted. And she said that Mr. Bragg was going to get a surprise. A surprise he won't like, I think."

Aunt Gladys nodded. "She'll fire him. Bragg made a big mistake when he said that Mrs. B. was a foolish old woman. She has some faults but being a fool isn't one of them." Ellen smiled. That was exactly what Mrs. B. had said about Aunt Gladys.

Her aunt didn't notice the smile. She went on. "But what about this forty dollars? How will Mrs. Kennedy come up with forty dollars? She won't make much more than that in a whole month."

"Mrs. B. said that the money must be paid by the end of the year. That's less than seven dollars a month." Ellen took a deep breath. "Joey and Charlene and I promised that we would figure out a way to come up with that money." As she said it, Ellen could feel doubt growing in her mind. Mama was frowning and Aunt Gladys was shaking her head.

"Well, I'm proud of you for wanting to help your friends, Ellen," said Mama. "But you should never promise more than you can do. You and Charlene are both busy already. Charlene has her brother and sister to look after and you have your house chores and the chickens."

"Oh, the chickens!" said Ellen. "They haven't been fed, have they?" She was glad to have a reason to stop trying to explain everything.

"Of course not," said Aunt Gladys. "Dishes I will do, but feed chickens I will *not*. You'll find some stale bread in a bowl on the counter." And she was off to her beautiful hidey-hole.

"And I have to go, too," said Mama. "We'll talk about this some more, Ellen." She picked up her shopping basket, ready to leave for Mrs. B.'s house, while Ellen went to apologize to the hens for bringing their breakfast late.

CHAPTER 17

When the chickens were fed Ellen went up to her room. She sat down at the little desk, took out the green and black notebook from the drawer, and opened it to the first page.

She read the word printed there: PLANS. Ellen stared at the word hoping some wonderful plan for making money would come into her mind. It didn't.

What Mama said was true. Charlene was busy all day looking after Gracie and Joey. She couldn't go out to work and neither could Joey.

"And neither can I. I can do jobs around the house and that helps Mama and then she can earn money." She closed the notebook and put it back in the drawer. "There's no way I can work and earn enough to help the Kennedys stay in the little house."

She shut the desk and got up. "I can think better in the tree. I'll make a sandwich and have my lunch out there."

She went to the kitchen, cut herself two pieces of bread, and made a sandwich of meatloaf left over from dinner yesterday. With that and an apple in her pocket, she could stay out in the tree for a good long time.

Soon she was sitting in her favourite place on the branch. The street was unusually quiet. The kids must be playing somewhere else, she thought. But the leaves around her rustled and she thought of Mrs. B. in her room full of green plants.

That's her green world, Ellen thought. But it's too quiet and there's no view at all. Mine is different.

She looked down at the bits of the neighbourhood she could see, and she listened to sounds coming from away down the street, people talking and a dog barking.

If I was under the tree I could see everything, she thought. I could knock on the Kennedys' front door and talk to Charlene. I'll eat my lunch and go down there when I'm finished.

She was halfway through the apple when she heard a voice below her.

"Little girl," it said. "I want you to give this to your mother."

Ellen stiffened. She knew that voice. It was trying to sound friendly but she recognized that deep and grating sound. It was Mr. Bragg.

She looked straight down. She could see the top of his head. He was wearing a grey felt hat, rather greasy looking around the brim, and he was standing on the sidewalk in front of the little house.

"Little girl," he said again. "I'm telling you to give this to your mother." His voice was growing impatient.

He must be talking to Gracie, thought Ellen. Where's Charlene? I'd better get down there.

Before she moved she looked down again and saw Mr. Bragg's arm reaching out. He was holding a piece of paper out toward the steps. Gracie must be sitting on the step where Ellen couldn't see her.

Ellen didn't stop to look any more. She got herself into her room and down the stairs in record time and hurried across the porch. Mr. Martineau was there, reading the newspaper. He didn't even look up. Then she was down the steps and standing in front of Mr. Bragg.

He stared at her with little blue eyes and said, "Just exactly who are you?"

Ellen didn't answer. She grabbed the paper out of his hand and looked at it. "EVICTION NOTICE" it said in big letters. Underneath were words like "delinquent rent," and "vacant possession," and a date. July 30th. One week away.

Ellen didn't read any more. Mr. Bragg was reaching for the piece of paper.

She clutched it to her so that he couldn't take it out of her hand. Behind her, Gracie was starting to cry.

Ellen turned toward the porch hoping that Charlene might appear, but all she saw was Gracie sitting on the top step with her hands over her eyes.

"I want him to go away," she wailed.

"It's all right, Gracie," Ellen said. "I'm going to get help."

But who could help her? It would take too long to get Aunt Gladys, and what might Mr. Bragg do while she was gone? She turned helplessly toward Saskatchewan House and suddenly knew what to do. Mr. Martineau. He was right on the front porch. And he was a lawyer!

Ellen called to him breathlessly, "Please help us, Mr. Martineau. This man—"

She didn't have to finish the sentence. Mr. Martineau was off the porch, across the front yard, and standing beside her. He took the piece of paper from her hand and glanced at it briefly. Then he stepped toward Mr. Bragg.

"Sir," he said. "This appears to be an eviction notice."

Mr. Bragg opened his mouth and closed it again. He took a step back.

"Stay where you are. I have a few things to say to you," said Mr. Martineau. "You are attempting to give this document to this small child here." He pointed to Gracie who had stopped crying and was staring with round eyes.

Mr. Bragg said nothing. He had beads of sweat on his forehead.

"Are you a police officer?" asked Mr. Martineau.

Mr. Bragg shook his head very slightly.

"Well then," said Mr. Martineau. "You have committed

three legal errors. I won't call them *crimes* but I could. First, you have tried to serve a legal document on a young child. Ridiculous. Second, an eviction order must be served by a police officer. You are not a police officer."

Mr. Bragg took another step backward.

"Don't move," ordered Mr. Martineau. "Third, and worst of all, this is not a legal eviction order. What you have is a piece of paper saying that this family will be evicted for non-payment of rent and that they must leave by a certain date. That's all it is—a piece of paper. There is nothing legal about it. You were trying to scare these people out of their home for some reason of your own."

Mr. Bragg finally managed to say something but his voice was scratchy, not the deep rumble Ellen had heard before.

"Who are you?" he demanded. "What right do you have to speak to me in such a way?"

"I am a lawyer," said Mr. Martineau. "I represent the law—and if you keep trying to drive these people from their home, I will see you in court."

He crumpled the paper into a ball, tossed it into the air, and caught it again. "This belongs in the trash," he said and stuck it in his pocket.

Then he turned and walked back to Saskatchewan House and sat down on the porch. But he did not pick up the newspaper. He stared at Mr. Bragg until Mr. Bragg retreated down the street. Ellen could tell that he was trying not to walk too fast.

"He doesn't want us to think he's running away," Ellen said to Gracie. "But that's what he's doing."

The front door of the little house opened and Charlene came out.

"I was just putting those precious clothes away," she said. "Not a rip in them, I'm glad to say."

She looked at Ellen and Gracie.

"What's going on here?" she asked. "Why do you both look as if you'd been running a race?"

"A man came," said Gracie. "He wanted to give me a piece of paper, but you told me and Mum told me not to take anything from a stranger. So I wouldn't take it. Then Ellen came and took the paper and she got that man over there and he came and told the man he shouldn't have done it."

She burst into tears again and Charlene sat down beside her and said, "It sounds like you did just the right thing. Now you can stop crying."

She looked at Ellen. "Now tell me your version of what happened."

Ellen sat down. "Mr. Bragg doesn't know that we talked to Mrs. B. He didn't want to wait a whole month to get you evicted with a proper notice. So he wrote up a fake eviction order to scare your family into running away. He tried to give it to Gracie. But thanks to Mr. Martineau over there, Mr. Bragg will definitely not be evicting you." She went on to tell Charlene exactly what Mr. Martineau had done.

Charlene got up and went over to the porch of Saskatchewan House. She stood in front of Mr. Martineau and held out her hand. The two of them shook hands and Charlene said, "When I grow up and have some money and need a lawyer, I'll come and find you. I know you're good. That Mr. Bragg, he thought he could scare anyone. But he couldn't scare you. Thanks."

"You are most welcome," said Mr. Martineau. "And I want to thank Ellen for giving me a chance to confront that ridiculous man. I guess I haven't forgotten how to be a lawyer. I *will* be seeing people in court again. That's for sure."

Charlene came back to her porch and sat down beside Gracie.

"But there's still a catch. We have to come up with forty dollars by the end of the year. We have six months. That's seven dollars each month. It might be impossible."

CHAPTER 18

The next morning Ellen woke up with the feeling that she was right on the edge of a dream that would tell her how to make money, but as she opened her eyes her dream melted. All she could remember was looking at a great pile of useless things. She couldn't even remember what was in the pile.

She ate breakfast with all the people of Saskatchewan House, but no one was in a talking mood. After breakfast Aunt Gladys talked even less than usual and went off to her hidey-hole wrapped in her own thoughts.

"Maybe the chickens will have something to say," Ellen said to herself. She picked up the bowl of scraps from the top of the icebox and went out to the garage. She was just tipping the scraps onto the garage floor when Joey opened the garden door and stepped into the garage.

He didn't say hello. He just asked, "Is that what they eat?"

"Mostly," said Ellen. "Not just bread but vegetable peelings and things like that. They aren't very fussy, and with ten people in the house we have plenty of scraps."

"There's a café up on Dupont Street that throws a lot of stuff away. Maybe I could collect it."

"You don't need to do that. These chickens have plenty to eat," said Ellen.

"They have a good place to live, too," said Joey. "Do they sleep in those boxes?"

"No," said Ellen. "That's where they lay eggs. They perch on that ladder over there to sleep. It's called roosting."

"How many eggs do they lay?" asked Joey.

"I usually get four eggs a day. Sometimes only three."

"Okay," said Joey. "Well, I've got to go get started." He opened the door and left.

Get started on what? Ellen shook her head. Joey never told you more than he had to. She checked to be sure the chickens had plenty of water. Then she looked in the nests and found four eggs.

"A good day," she said. "Thank you, chickens."

Ellen went into the house and put the eggs in the egg bowl in the icebox. She went through the kitchen to the bottom of the stairs and started to go up to her room as she usually did in the mornings, but on the landing she stopped.

"I need to talk to Charlene," she said out loud. "Sitting in the tree won't help us figure out how to earn forty dollars."

She went back downstairs and out the front door. Charlene and Gracie were sitting on the steps of the little house. Ellen went over and sat down, too. No one said a word.

Joey came around the side of the house. His face and

shirt were streaked with dirt, but he looked very pleased with himself.

"Whatever have you been doing?" said Charlene. "You look as if you've been rolling in dirt."

"I've been cleaning out the garage," said Joey with great satisfaction.

Charlene stared at him.

"Have you gone crazy?" she asked.

"No," said Joey. "I have an idea, but we need a clean garage to make it work. I pushed all the junk over into the corner so now there's plenty of room."

"Room for what?"

Ellen looked at Joey and suddenly knew exactly what he was going to say.

"Chickens," said Joey.

Charlene stared at Joey. "You think we could have chickens in our garage? Like over at Saskatchewan House?"

"Sure," said Joey. "Why not? And then we could sell the eggs! That would make us some money."

"Yes," said Charlene. She was quiet for a minute. "It might work. Would you help us, Ellen? You know about chickens."

"I'd help," said Ellen. Suddenly, she felt excited instead of discouraged. "And I bet I know where we could get chickens. From Al and Tony. That's where Aunt Gladys got ours."

"But we'd have to pay for them," said Charlene. "Don't

forget about that. We already don't have any money."

Ellen jumped up. "Wait," she said. "I'll be right back."

She hurried up to her room and opened the little drawer in the desk. She took out the notebook and the four one-dollar bills and ran back to Charlene and Joey.

"Look," she said. "My dad sent me this money. We can buy some chickens. I'll talk to Tony and Al and find out how many hens we can get."

"We can't spend your money," protested Charlene. "You might need it for something special."

"My dad said to do something good with it," said Ellen. "This is something good. I want to buy chickens! Later on, when Mrs. B. has her money you can share your eggs with Saskatchewan House. We never have enough."

"That makes sense," said Charlene. "Thanks, Ellen. But the chickens are only the beginning. If we get them they need stuff. Like food and a place to sleep and…"

Joey interrupted. "I'll get scraps from the café up on Dupont. They throw away lots of things chickens will eat. And I'll get boxes from up at Casa Loma. You saw all that wood. No one wants it and we need it."

"Okay," said Charlene. "Let's say we can get chickens and feed them, and they lay eggs. Who is going to buy our eggs? People can get eggs at the corner store."

Ellen had an idea about that. "The people up on the hill

would buy them. I know they would. We have to make a little sign to leave at their doors telling them that we have eggs for sale. I bet they would buy all your hens can lay."

"Well, I could make the signs," said Charlene. "I don't know anything about taking care of chickens, but I could draw a nice picture. And my printing is good."

"It is," said Joey. "She always wins prizes with her penmanship."

Charlene looked surprised at this praise, but she said, "We have to keep track of everything. I mean how many eggs we sell and how much we charge and all that."

Ellen took the little notebook out of her pocket.

"Look," she said. "We can write everything down here. It even says 'PLANS' on the first page." She opened the book and showed them.

"Where did you get that?" asked Joey.

"It was waiting for me in the desk when I came to Saskatchewan House," said Ellen. "I didn't know what to do with it then, but now it's just what we need." She turned to the next page and printed *Do First*.

"Well, first we have to get the stuff from Casa Loma," said Joey. "I can do that, but it would be good if you came, too, Ellen. You know the sort of stuff we'll need."

Ellen thought about the watchman. Then she thought about the money they had to earn.

"Okay," she said. "We should go tomorrow. In the morning." She didn't want to meet Mama coming down the hill on her way home from work.

"Oh yeah," said Joey. "Morning will be better."

"Gracie and I will finish cleaning out the garage," said Charlene. "And Ellen, you'll have to find out how many chickens we can get for four dollars."

"I'll ask about it at dinner tonight," said Ellen. "But now it must be lunch time. All this planning is making me very hungry." And she went back to Saskatchewan House feeling that a plan was a very encouraging thing.

CHAPTER 19

Ellen heated up some tomato soup and ate it at the dining room table. While she ate, she thought about buying chickens and selling eggs. How much money could they really make?

She washed her bowl and spoon and went out on the front porch. As she hoped, Mr. Martineau had left his copy of the *Globe and Mail* beside the wicker chair. She sat down and began to look for an advertisement for groceries.

She found what she was looking for in an Eaton's grocery department ad. Thirty-nine cents for one dozen eggs, it said.

"Thirty-nine cents," Ellen thought. "We'll have to sell an awful lot of eggs to make forty dollars."

She went up to her room and took out her scribbler.

"We might get eight hens," she said to herself. "Then we could surely count on two dozen eggs a week. Maybe a few more."

She went on figuring. Multiplication always took her a long time, and she had to do it several times to be sure she had got it right, but in the end she knew. If they could sell two dozen eggs a week, by the end of December they would have twenty dollars and twenty-eight cents.

"That's only half of what we need," she said out loud. "How can we earn twenty more dollars?"

There was no one to answer, and Ellen didn't feel like rushing down to share this discouraging news with Charlene and Joey and Gracie, so she left her pages of smudged numbers on the bed and opened the window.

The tree seemed to welcome her. She sat on the big branch and didn't move for a minute. All around her the leaves stirred gently. Then she scooted along the branch until she felt that she was in the very middle of the tree, her own place in the tree world.

"I can't climb higher. The branches are too far apart. And I can't jump down. I'm up too high. When I'm here, I'm just here. It is my place and I like it, but I can't stay here very long."

Looking down she could see the top of Charlene's head as she sat on the bottom step, and she could hear Gracie showing Jeanette how good she was at hopping. Now she knew just how Gracie looked. She also knew that Charlene was wishing that someone her own age would come over and talk with her.

Ellen looked around at the green world of the tree. The light coming through the leaves was gentle and there was a soft rustling sound, almost like breathing.

"I'll come back when I can," she promised the listening tree. "I'll come back because I like it here. But I don't need to listen any more."

When she turned to go back to the house, Ellen saw her mother standing at the open window. She couldn't see whether she was smiling or just waiting.

She scooted herself along the branch and came across the roof. Mama stepped away from the window so that Ellen could come inside. Then she said, "I'm home a bit early." She put her hand on Ellen's shoulder. "Now I know where you've been spending some of your time."

"Yes," said Ellen. "I have spent a lot of time in the tree. It's like the loft in the barn back home. Sometimes I just wanted to be in the loft by myself. I could do anything or nothing. No one would know. It felt like my place. Here in Saskatchewan House nothing was mine until I found the tree."

"I know," said Mama. "It has felt pretty strange to me, too. I don't know why I thought it would be easy for you. It wasn't, was it?"

Ellen shook her head. "I couldn't just go out and play with the kids. You wanted me to, but I couldn't. The tree helped."

"Your dad would like your tree. And I guess it's his fault that you knew how to go out on that branch." Mama smiled. "You'll write to him about it, won't you?"

"Oh yes," said Ellen. "And I have to tell him about how I'm going to use the money he sent. I told you that me and Charlene and Joey have to come up with enough to pay the Kennedys' back rent, right?"

Mama nodded and Ellen went on, "I'm going to use the four dollars to buy some chickens from Al and Tony. Then we'll sell the eggs." She looked at her mother for a moment. "Dad said I should use the money to do something good. Do you think he would like our plan?"

Mama smiled a little. "Mike would probably do the same thing if he could, and you and I already have what we need." She patted Ellen on the shoulder. "You're putting a lot of faith in chickens, you know."

But Ellen was still thinking about eggs. "Do you think the people in the big houses up by the castle will buy eggs from us?"

"Mrs. B. will, I'm sure. She eats a poached egg every morning. And I'll ask about the neighbours. It's not as if you'll have dozens to sell."

Ellen suddenly remembered about the price of eggs. "Mama, I have to go talk to Charlene." She pointed to her scribbler full of multiplication figures. "You're right. The chickens might not be enough."

Mama gave her a little hug. "Maybe you won't be spending so much time in the tree now," she said. "I think you are going to be very busy."

Ellen picked up her scribbler and went downstairs and over to the Kennedys' porch. Charlene saw what Ellen was holding in her hand.

"You've been figuring, too," she said.

"Yes," said Ellen. "I found out that we can sell our eggs for about forty cents a dozen. No more. So even if we're very, very lucky we'll only make about half of what we need. Is that what you got?"

Charlene nodded. "I know that getting the money we need won't be easy. At least half is better than nothing. We'll just have to find something else we can do."

"So we'll go on with the chickens?"

"Yes. And go on with them after the rent is paid. Then we can eat the eggs and share them with your house, too."

She looked so pleased that Ellen decided to give up worrying until the next day when she would go up to Casa Loma with Joey.

"Let's get Pearl and Jeanette and play a game of freeze tag," she said. And that is what they did.

That night at dinner, Ellen asked Al and Tony how many chickens she could buy for four dollars.

"You want laying hens, right?" said Al.

"Yes, we need enough hens to lay two dozen eggs a week," said Ellen.

"Who's going to eat all those eggs?" asked Tony. "Al and I could do it, but I don't suppose you're getting the chickens for us, and there are already six hens out in the garage."

"These are for the Kennedys next door," said Ellen.

"Charlene and Joey and I are going to sell the eggs." And she told the Third Floor Boys all about the plan.

"For such an important plan, we'll make you a special deal," said Al. "We usually sell our hens for fifty cents, but just this once we'll throw in an extra. That will give you a better chance of getting two dozen eggs in a week. We don't make any promises, mind you. Hens do as they like. But if you treat them well, they just might do what you want them to."

Ellen went to sleep that night hoping for cooperative hens and a new money-making idea.

CHAPTER 20

The next morning Joey showed up in the garage while Ellen was feeding the chickens. He had a canvas bag over his shoulder.

"When we go up to the castle we want to carry away as much as we can," he said. "Do you have a bag like this?"

"Of course I don't," said Ellen. "We're going to look for boxes for the hens to lay their eggs in, and some broomsticks or something like that for them to roost on. None of that would fit in your bag anyway."

"We might find something else," said Joey.

"We're not taking just anything we happen to see," said Ellen. "I'm not going to be a thief."

"You'll see," said Joey. "I'm not a thief, either. But no one at the castle wants anything that's there. So why not take it?"

Ellen didn't answer. She poured water from her bucket into the chickens' pan and found three eggs in the nests.

Then she said, "I told Aunt Gladys that I was going up to Casa Loma with you. She knows we need stuff for your chickens, so she said okay, but I can't go anywhere else without telling her."

"At least you can come to the castle," said Joey. "When Charlene asked Mum if she and Gracie could come along, Mum just said no." He shook his head. "Of course Gracie told her that she came with us the other day and then we had to explain everything."

"Was your mum very mad?" asked Ellen.

"Well, she started to be, but we explained that your aunt knew we were going and how important it was, and then she wasn't mad. But she said that Gracie is too young for such adventures. So Charlene can't come today."

"Too bad," said Ellen. "Next time I'll stay with Gracie. We'd better get going, Joey. I'll see you out front. I have to put these eggs in the icebox first."

As she walked up Bathurst Street beside Joey, Ellen thought about the wall around the castle. She wasn't worried about climbing it, but how would they get boards and boxes over? They came to the door in the wall, and Joey stopped, though Ellen could see that it was closed tight. He grinned, reached out, and gave it a shove. It opened.

"Look," he said and showed her that the latch inside was held up by a stick left in just the right place.

"Did it last time I was here. It saves time. No one else knows about it so they'll think the gate is latched."

Ellen made a face. It certainly was much easier to go in through the door, but surely someone ought to care about keeping people out of the castle garden.

By now they were making their way along the wall, and Ellen was too busy pushing branches out of her face to worry about the door any more. Joey headed straight for the pile of wood and bits of metal and crockery heaped against one end of the terrace.

Ellen looked at the heap and remembered her dream about piles of useless stuff. Surely this pile could not hold the answer to their problem! But she could already see some shallow boxes that would make good nests. When she pulled one of them out of the heap, some small dented saucepans toppled over. No one would want them. Under them was a teakettle with holes in it and some twisted trays made of tin.

"There's a lot of metal stuff in here," she said to Joey, who was stacking up a few short boards and another good box.

"Yeah," he said. "I don't think any of it is any good."

"No," said Ellen. "Not to us—but don't people melt down old metal and do something with it?"

Joey stopped poking in the pile and looked at her. "Yes," he said. "There's a scrap metal place on Dupont. Brian and I took a bundle of wire there. It was in his uncle's garage. They gave us twenty-five cents. There's a lot more metal here than that bunch of wire." He turned to her and almost shouted, "We can sell it! All we have to do is carry it to the scrap yard. We can sell it!"

"We can't just take a whole lot of metal without asking," said Ellen. "We have to ask."

As she said it, she knew that Joey would never ask. To him, the garden of Casa Loma was *his*. No one else seemed to care about it—so why shouldn't he take whatever he needed and wanted? But Ellen knew she couldn't just walk off with metal that was worth money.

"We have to ask," she said again.

"Who are you going to ask?" said Joey. "The castle doesn't really belong to anyone except the city, and the city doesn't even want it. I guess you could go down to City Hall."

"There's a watchman, isn't there? We saw him the other day. I'm going to ask him. If he says go to City Hall, I'll go to City Hall."

She walked away from the trash pile until she came to some steps that led up to the terrace. Joey stared after her but he didn't follow. He turned back to the heap.

Ellen stood on the terrace, wondering which was the proper entrance to the castle. It was hard to tell what was a door and what was a window. She was thinking of trying to walk around the building to the street side when suddenly, one of the tall windows opened like a door and a man stepped out.

"Hey there, little lady," he said. "What are you doing here? This building is closed."

Ellen knew that she should answer, but she was so

surprised by the man's appearance that it took her a minute to speak. He was tall and wearing denim jeans, a black shirt frayed around the cuffs, a wide-brimmed hat, and worn leather boots. His face was deeply tanned.

"Who are you?" asked Ellen—and then realized that she had no right to ask that question.

"The real question is, who are you?" said the man.

"My name is Ellen and I live down the hill, but I come from Saskatchewan, near Moose Jaw." The words just came out, but at the same time she wondered why she was even mentioning Saskatchewan.

"Well, that's why you look so familiar. I come from Alberta, near Medicine Hat. My name is Ray. I guess we used to be almost neighbours."

"Do you live in the castle?"

"I do. I'm the new watchman. I've been out east looking for work. No luck, so I hopped the train heading west and got off in Toronto. I guess my luck has changed because I talked my way into this job in a castle! You just never know where you'll end up."

"I know," said Ellen, thinking of the boarding house on Manning Avenue.

"Now, since I'm the watchman, I'd like to know what you are doing here in the garden of Casa Loma."

Ellen took a deep breath.

"Well, my friends who live next door have to earn some money to pay their back rent, so they are going to raise chickens and sell the eggs. I know about chickens so I'm helping them. We just need a few things from the trash pile so we can build nests. That's what we were doing but then—"

Joey's voice interrupted her. He came running up the steps, talking at the same time.

"It's me and my two sisters and my mum who might get evicted," he said and came to a stop beside Ellen. "And the chickens won't get us enough money. So, Mr. Ray, sir, could we take away the junk metal stuff that's in that pile down there? We could sell it and that would help us not be evicted."

"You and Ellen would take this metal?"

"Probably my friend Brian would help. Ellen has to get the chickens going."

"You are certainly enterprising young folks," said Ray.

"We have to earn forty dollars by the end of the year," said Joey. "If we don't..." He stopped talking and shook his head.

"Ah," said Ray, sadly. "Eviction shouldn't happen to a cat, let alone to a nice young fellow like you. Well, I give you permission to take away what you and your buddy Brian can carry that's in that trash pile. Just the two of you, you understand—and keep it quiet. I don't want this place to be overrun with looters. The city wants something left to tear down, if that's what they decide to do."

"Thanks, Ray," said Ellen. She turned to go but then she turned back. "I'm glad I met you. When I saw you I knew you must be from the west, somewhere."

"Did you, now?" said Ray. "I guess the hat gave me away. Now you go on down and get what you need for the chickens. I'll be watching for the metal pickers." He looked straight at Joey. "Don't go thinking I won't know you're there."

Joey looked down at his feet and then up again. "Thank you, sir," he said.

Ray smiled at the children and stepped back through the tall window.

Joey looked at Ellen. "Wait till we tell Charlene about Ray," he said. "I'll bet she won't believe us."

The two of them went back to the trash pile and picked up the boxes and boards they had found. It was time to go home.

CHAPTER 21

When Ellen and Joey got back to the little house, they found Charlene in the garage piling up old shingles as neatly as she could.

"I sent Gracie down the street to play with Glenda. She's not much help with this job." She looked at the boards and boxes they were carrying. "It looks like you got some good stuff."

"It's good," said Joey, "but not as good as what we have to tell you. Come on. Sit on the steps and listen."

When Joey and Ellen were finished, Charlene shook her head and said, "Last week, I wouldn't have believed that someone like Ray would be living in Casa Loma, but I've gotten so I believe almost anything. If the metal that's in the trash pile will help us make the forty dollars, I'm happy. That's all."

She got up and walked over to Saskatchewan House and back again. Then she said, "Everything that's happened this week is almost unbelievable. Those men trying to get us evicted, us going to talk to Mrs. B., getting chickens so they can lay eggs in the garage. It's all just crazy. But I know it happened."

She came back to the steps and said, almost to herself,

"But there is one thing I still don't understand."

She looked at Ellen for a long minute, and went on, "You heard Mr. Bragg and that other man talking one night. That's how it all began. You heard them say that they were going to get us out of our house. It's a good thing you did because if you hadn't heard them, we might be flitting tonight. But where were you when you heard them? That's what I want to know."

Ellen tried to interrupt but Charlene went right on. "They certainly didn't want anyone to hear them, so they would have been looking around. If you had been on the porch they would have seen you. And you couldn't have heard them from your room. My room's right up there."

She pointed at the bay window over the porch. "I've tried to hear what people are saying in front of the house but I can only make out a word or two. *You* heard a whole conversation. So where were you?"

"I was going to tell you," said Ellen. "But things kept happening. You see—"

Joey interrupted. "I know where you were."

Ellen stared at him. "You couldn't know," she said.

Joey got up and went over to the listening tree. He put his hand on its trunk.

"You were up in this tree," he said.

Ellen couldn't believe it. "How did you know?"

"I needed a good stick to make a slingshot one day, so I was looking at all the trees on the street. I guess you didn't see me. But when I looked up in this tree, I saw feet. Two feet dangling in the air. So I knew someone was sitting on a branch up there. After that I looked for those feet and sometimes I saw them."

"Why didn't you tell me?" said Charlene indignantly. "You should have told me."

"Why?" said Joey. "I figured it must be that new girl who had just come to live in Saskatchewan House." He looked at Ellen. "I already knew you didn't want to play." He grinned. "That was okay with me. I knew you'd come down sooner or later."

Ellen was amazed. "I thought no one could see me," she said. "I thought I was invisible."

"You just forgot about your feet," said Charlene.

Ellen said, "Thanks for not telling anyone, Joey. I just felt like being invisible for a while."

Now Joey looked embarrassed. "I've got to go find Brian and tell him about what we're going to do up at the castle," he said and ran off down the street.

Ellen and Charlene looked after him.

"You never know about Joey," said Charlene. "Is it nice up in that tree?"

"It's like a green room," said Ellen. "The leaves move all the time, just gently, and you can only see little bits of the world outside the tree." She looked down at the splintery porch step. "I listened to you and Joey and everyone. I felt so strange here those first days and the tree gave me a chance to know something about you. Do you mind that I was listening?"

"What did you hear? Just me bossing Gracie around and yelling at Joey. I don't care about that." She paused and then went on. "But now that I know about it, I wouldn't like to think you might be up there listening. I'd have to watch what I said." She made a face and laughed.

"I won't listen anymore," said Ellen. "I don't need to. It's way more fun to be with you and Joey and Gracie down on the ground."

"That reminds me," said Charlene, jumping up. "I have to go get Gracie. I'll see you later."

Ellen watched her go off toward Jeanette's house. Then she went over to the listening tree and looked up into its branches. They rose high over her head, and the trunk felt strong when she put her hand against it.

"A tree can be a friend," she said to herself. "Whether I'm up in it or not."

Ellen went into Saskatchewan House and up to her little room to write a letter to her dad—all about the chickens and the castle and Charlene, Joey, and Gracie. And especially about the listening tree.

HISTORICAL NOTE

The Great Depression, which lasted from 1929 to the late 1930s, was a time of great economic difficulty that affected many countries around the world. Banks and businesses failed, and thousands upon thousands of people found themselves unemployed and unable to provide for their families.

The Depression hit Canada particularly hard. In the Prairies there were several years of drought, crops failed, and many farmers were forced into bankruptcy. When the price of wheat dropped, many of these farmers had to leave their land to look for work.

It wasn't just the countryside that fell on hard times, however, as urban centres were also affected. Any area that was dependent on certain trades had a difficult time in the Depression. The Prairies were dependent on farms, but cities like Toronto were dependent on industry, and when people had no money to spend for goods, many jobs disappeared. In an attempt to help its citizens find jobs, the Government of Canada started a Public Works campaign that got people working on highways, dams, and bridges. During this time, the 400-series of highways was built. To this day, the 401 remains one of the busiest stretches of highway in North America.

For people who managed to find jobs, wages were low,

and it was difficult to stay out of debt. At that time, most women stayed at home to care for their children, but during the Depression they sometimes found themselves working outside the home in order to pay the bills, as Ellen's mother and Charlene's mother do in *The Listening Tree*. The older children were often left to look after themselves and their younger brothers and sisters.

A good way for children like Ellen, Joey, and Charlene to raise money to help their families was to collect things that people dropped or threw away, like the metal that they found at Casa Loma. A glass bottle could bring three cents, while scrap metal could bring a lot more. People at that time became resourceful in order to survive.

Casa Loma, the abandoned castle in this story, was the dream home of Sir Henry Pellatt. He lived there with his wife for ten years, but he made poor business decisions and had to move out of his castle in 1924. People had many ideas about what to do with Casa Loma, including turning it into a hotel, but because of the Depression, none of the plans worked out. In the end, the City of Toronto took possession of the run-down castle for unpaid taxes. Casa Loma stood vacant until 1936 when the Kiwanis Club offered to lease it and turn it into a tourist attraction. Today, thousands of sightseers visit Casa Loma each year to admire the dream castle that Sir Henry Pellatt built.